ASPEN INCIDENT

ASPEN INCIDENT

Tom Murphy

St. Martin's Press,
New York

 For information, write:
St. Martin's Press, Inc., 175 Fifth Ave.,
New York, N.Y. 10010.
Manufactured in the United States of America

Library of Congress Cataloging in Publication Data

Murphy, Tom, 1935—
Aspen incident.

I. Title.
PZ4.M9789As [PS3563.U762] 813'.5'4 78-4363
ISBN 0-312-05728-8

This book is for all the Connors,
skiing and non-skiing:
Ruth Ann, Jim, Cathy, Jimmy
and Patricia, with love.

ASPEN INCIDENT

1

You never rode a chair lift with a dead man. It stays with you, the feeling, part shock and part fear, gut vibrating like banjo strings because you're hanging there trapped in the bright sky over Aspen with nothing more than hope and half an inch of goosedown parka between you and the next bullet, and all the while the lifeblood of a man you hardly know falls sparkling fifty feet to the virgin snow.

A senator's blood is just like yours and mine, red and sticky, and when a certain amount of it spills out, he dies. I didn't need to know that.

For me the killing of Senator Blake Ross, Democrat, Pennsylvania, began on a slow Thursday night in Joe's Place.

Joe's Place is a bar, with food. In any ski town you'll find a few special places where the good people go, the locals, the racers and instructors and their girls, where people go because they want to be together in a friendly room, because they avoid the kind of see-and-be-seen establishments where the name of the game is let's-all-impress-each-other. Aspen's a good town, or anyway it used to be, before the glitter people came in. And Aspen still has some good places, if you know where to look. The Red Onion, for one, and the bar at the Hotel Jerome. And Joe's Place. That's fine by me. I'm Joe.

Joe Bird, Proprietor: that has a nice ring to it. Not as nice, maybe, as Joe Bird, Olympic Downhill Gold Medalist might have had, but that's another story and it's packed away safely on that hidden shelf where good dreams go when you turn thirty, which for me was nearly six years ago and hurting.

Thursday, second week of February, around eleven at night. It was a typical crowd, a typical mid-season night. Joe's Place was amply filled but not mobbed: an easygoing bunch of regulars. Sometimes, on a Saturday, it gets a little more hilarious than I like. One reason I'm here in the middle of some of the biggest mountains God ever thought of is the quiet. Well, that Thursday was a quiet bunch. Mostly I get a wine-and-beer crowd. Now and then a five-martini-type person will wander in by mistake, but to tell the truth, the really heavy drinkers find a warmer welcome elsewhere.

The "JOE'S PLACE" on the door means what it says. I want it the way I want it, and I guess it's lucky enough people agree with me to make it pay.

Thursday night in February, in Aspen, Colorado. There was nothing more on my mind than whether to ski Ajax Mountain first thing tomorrow or Snowmass. We were getting a couple of inches of new snow, tiny little pinpoint flakes that make Aspen powder at its best almost indistinguishable from talcum. Snow alerts were going off inside me: small buzzings and tinglings and a kind of caged-in feeling that must be something like the way a junkie feels when he's out of smack. I faced it long ago: Joe Bird is hooked on skiing, deeply, irrevocably, hopelessly, climb-the-glacier-in-July, fly-to-Chile-in-August, desperately addicted to the slopes. Even though it's crazy and I'm not. Even though my right knee is held together by nylon and willpower, and my skiing is only a pale crippled ghost of what it was in my racing days. I'll never learn.

Joe's Place is a ramshackle old Victorian house with most of the parlor floor gutted into one big room. There's a long mahogany bar, a fireplace, and tables that seat about thirty. The decor is Early Neglect, but there's a real pressed-tin ceiling, and the wood in the floorboards is mellow, and between the fire and the fat red candles on every table it's a welcoming place.

Down from the weathered-pine walls looks my antique harem: faded sepia-tone photographs in which some of the West's naughtier ladies gaze enticingly out of an era when men were men and women knew what to do about it. Here in prim black frames are game old girls like Belle Starr, Two Gun Sally Patterson, Calamity Jane, and Lily Cigar.

Thursday night in February.

Two ski bums tending bar, Charlie and Rick, were doing fine. Charlie's a huge, bearlike kid with a lot of brown hair and very few inhibitions and a grin slightly wider than Independence Pass. Rick's another animal altogether, quiet, wiry, and sleek, crack skier, flawed cynic, his very well-educated voice making jokes while his dark haunted eyes try not to think about the time when he'll have to go back East and take over about half the real estate in Philadelphia, closely held these two hundred and some years by Rick's family, whose name was so famous that even I had heard it. They're good kids, Ricky and Charlie. "Ski bum" is not a put-down word in ski country. It just implies a certain excess of dedication, a kind of happy-go-skiing priesthood above the timberline. These kids often give up everything to ski. You have to admire that, especially if you're me. Because I'd be doing the same thing if luck hadn't let me buy Joe's Place.

Anyway, Charlie and Rick had the wine and beer flowing good, and Rita—that's Rita Tyler—was waiting table in her usual easygoing, eye-boggling style.

People's eyes boggled at Rita because Rita is one of the great natural wonders of Colorado, and completely unaffected by it. She's a tall girl, maybe an inch shorter than my six feet, with an absolutely real waterfall of sun-streaked blond hair and a body that somehow manages to be ripe and contained at the same time and a face with possibly a shade too much chin to fit on a cameo, but head-turning beautiful nevertheless, eyes set wide and colored in a disconcerting gray-green the Chinese call celadon, and all this wrapped up in a sense of humor that could look at all five sides of a situation and laugh at four of them. You could get very fond of Rita Tyler, especially if you were me. Rita was one of the main attractions of Joe's Place. She could even ski.

A quiet Thursday in February. Al Coggin was nursing a beer and telling me one more time how his kid won that week's giant slalom in the thirteen-to-fifteen-year-old class. Al didn't have to nurse his beer. Al is one of Aspen's Finest, our six-man local law enforcers, and no lawman can pick up a check in Joe's Place. If my conversation with Al was gliding along on automatic pilot, it wasn't Al's fault. He's a good man, Al, and a good cop, seldom as we need policework in Aspen. Al Coggin is tall as a mountain spruce and as straight, home-grown in Aspen. Al doesn't say much except on two subjects: his ski-crazed kid, Sandy, whom I coach from time to time, a decent kid with glimmerings of real potential. Al's other subject is less fun, and that's his running war of nerves with his boss, our worthy sheriff, Billy Medina. I don't take sides, but I see more of Al than I do of Billy, so that's the side I hear. But tonight, thank God, the subject was Sandy.

"That's fine, Al. He's come a long way this season."

Al swirled the last inch of beer in his mug and I signaled Rita for a refill for him and more red wine for me. But I never got to hear exactly how far young Sandy Coggin had come that season, because right about then the front door swept open and a great wave of charisma poured in, followed by the junior senator from Pennsylvania and his lovely wife, Martha.

They used those very words, and the words had reached across time and all the big mountains and other thoughts and other women I had put between the memory of her and me, even knowing all those years you can't do that: they don't make mountains big enough, or strong-enough wine. "*The lovely Martha Ross gave a speech today in flawless Spanish to the Spanish-speaking community of Philadelphia.*" Sometimes they thought of other words. Sometimes Martha was gracious, or charming; once, if I remember right, she was even philanthropic. But always she was Martha, in all the media, newspapers, the big picture news magazines, TV. I'd seen her name, her picture, and his in a hundred newspapers and magazines, and if I were more of a reader the hundreds might well have been millions: they were the hot young stars in the liberal Democratic firmament. It was nearly three years to the next presidential election, and already the press was running out of adjectives to praise them.

Well, you'd expect it of Martha.

And now Martha stood there on my old worn floorboards, small, straight, that tiny perfect head poised expectantly on a long slender neck, the polished dark-walnut hair pulled back behind the delicate symmetry of her face, chin up as always, the huge gray eyes taking in the warmth and color of Joe's Place with the gentle unstated confidence of someone to whom a lot of good things had already happened, and a lot of even better things were going to happen very soon.

There was always something disarming in her air of sure expectation. She had the unconscious selfishness of very young children on the night before Christmas, eyes bright with visions that were no less real for being too perfect ever to come true on this less-than-perfect planet, touching and lovely and doomed.

For a minute I stood there gaping, fighting a kid's impulse to run and hide. Then some kind of reflex took over and I excused myself from Al Coggin, got up, and managed to negotiate the five miles of uncharted minefields that filled the twenty feet of floor between us.

Martha Edwards had come a long way from Eagle Grove, Kansas. So had I.

"Hi, Martha."

"Why . . . it's Joe! Joe Bird. This is a surprise."

Her voice was a little deeper than I remembered. The timbre and tone of it had gone from something light and watercolor and kind of floating to richer, more vibrant. I didn't analyze it then, but what had happened was that her voice was trained now, a voice used to giving speeches, capable of filling large rooms with its own soft authority. She continued.

"People told us this is the place . . . Joe's Place . . . but, good heavens! We had no idea you'd be the Joe! You're looking very well, Joe."

I guess I looked as well as you can expect a man to look when he's just stepped off solid ground and into a bottomless crevasse.

"It's been a long time." I drew the banality around me like a magic cloak, hoping that it could make me invisible, praying I wouldn't actually start bleeding right here in the middle of Joe's Place.

"Hasn't it?" she said, taking my arm with a butterfly's touch. "Much, much too long. Blake, honey, here is an old, old friend. Joe Bird. Joe, Blake. My husband." There was something endearing in this, in the suggestion I might not know who Blake Ross was, or the name of the man she'd married.

"It's good to meet you, Senator." Blake Ross took my hand, and you'd have to work to guess that mine was maybe the hundredth hand he had shaken that day.

Blake gave me his hundred-karat smile, and even his big wide-set brown eyes smiled, something rare in politicians.

But then, Blake Ross was no ordinary politician. A lot of

very smart money was betting that Mr. and Mrs. Blake Ross would be at home at number 1600 Pennsylvania Avenue in Washington in three years. You didn't have to be psychic to figure out why.

Think of any natural-born leader you ever knew, multiply that by ten, the special quality all leaders have, and I'm here to tell you Blake Ross had more of it.

Start with looks. There is such a thing as a beautiful man, and Blake was that, and in spades. Tall, six-three easy, with a pure WASP face all planes and crags and the famous profile just waiting for its coin, plenty of tumbledown brown hair with plenty of Noble Roman forehead to tumble down, deep brown eyes set wide, that interballistic smile, a laugh you remembered, a voice you didn't forget. Blake Ross made you think of quick soaring things, of races won and the flights of eagles and wind straining at spinnakers.

Blake Ross could have been selling snake oil or dreams, leading the Children's Crusade or a bank robbery: it didn't matter. There were things in the man to make you want to go where he was going, anywhere, the sooner the better.

You chose well, Martha.

If ever jealousy had been going to get Joe Bird, it would have been there and then. But I had no more business envying Blake Ross than a kitchen match has being jealous of the sun. Not of what he was, nor of what he had. In taking Martha Edwards, Blake took nothing that I owned or even had the smallest claim to, except in dreams, where for no logical reason it seems to hurt the most.

So Blake Ross had it all: the looks, the brains, the charisma, and the fine old family name. And now he had Martha and Martha's money, in case his own ever ran out, which by all accounts was very unlikely.

It isn't easy to like the man who got the only girl you ever really wanted. Blake Ross made it easy, as he made all things seem easy. The sure sign of a pro.

"Listen," he said, and I listened: "let's can the 'Senator' stuff, Joe. We came out here to get away from all that."

Martha took my arm. "An old pal of Daddy's," she said, "lent us his house in Snowmass. But the truth is, we're shopping. If it turns out we like it, we may even build here." *Vail,* I prayed inside my numbing brain, *let them find Vail. Vail is for politicians.* Aspen is a very small town, despite the glitter people with their Mercedeses and cocaine and indoor whirlpool baths, and I like to think of it as my town, at least partly. I have more than money invested in Aspen. But if Martha was moving in, it could just happen that Joe Bird might have to move on.

"Whose house?" I asked it mechanically.

Blake answered for her. "Martha's Uncle Austin. Austin Pierce." He said it casually, as though the name was just another name, with no legends attached.

Martha smiled as we all sat down at a corner table. "He's such an old sweetie, not really an uncle, of course, I've just always called him that. Did you ever meet Uncle Austin in the old days, Joe? He was forever coming to visit Daddy."

"I don't recall him from home. But I have met the man a few times out here." *Sweetie* would not have been the word I'd use to describe old Austin Pierce, but then, I didn't really know the man. Twice, maybe, we'd met for a few minutes at parties. He wasn't a Joe's Place type at all—if there is such a thing. We're not nearly fancy enough for the Austin Pierce set. He was s special breed, was Martha's old sweetie.

Austin Pierce was the result of big Texas money put through so many fancy filters you had to look closely to find the Texas in him, what with Eastern prep schools and Harvard and serving time in the State Department.

Pierce looked and sounded more like Wall Street than sagebrush, and what he was doing in Aspen was anyone's guess. He was a round soft man of maybe sixty, with thin pink skin and a jolly laugh that seemed never to extend to his eyes. Pierce collected Japanese art and influence, and he'd built a huge stone-and-glass house at Snowmass, the highest up the mountain, jutting into the ski trails like some great rock battleship, a huge American flag flying at all times from the terrace. Austin Pierce played in the backyards of power and probably had some power himself. Right now he was in some fairly impressive Washington job, undersecretary of something-or-other, I could never remember of just what. You never saw the man on skis.

"Joe?" It was Rita with my wine. I wondered how long she'd been standing there.

"Thanks."

Rita smiled her nice slow smile and injected a much-needed touch of reality into the situation.

"Martha, Senator Ross, meet Rita Tyler." How very beautiful. I was capable of uttering simple sentences. A miracle had happened. Pressing my luck, I asked them what they'd like to drink.

"I'd like a Coke." That much of Eagle Grove had stayed with Martha. I wondered if anything else had.

"I'll have a Coors," added Blake with the supple ease of one who knows the best local produce anywhere. Rita moved toward the bar, and he added, "That's some lady."

"She's a good one." She was also my lady, but they didn't need to know that.

"Local talent?"

"She grew up in Boston."

"Maybe I ought to give Boston another chance." Blake's laugh flowed out of him warm and bubbling, surrounding me, making me part of his magic circle. "*Sure, fella,*" the laugh seemed to say, "*we're all pals here, old fraternity brothers after a few beers.*" It wasn't true, but for a moment I believed it because he made me want to believe it. I smiled, and raised my wineglass in a silent toast, and found myself wondering what else this man could make me believe.

"Joe!" Martha had a way of saying things in small, urgent exclamations, charming explosions of interest and enthusiasm. I could still catch ripples of Kansas in her voice now that she's relaxed a little, now that we were all close in our corner table. She went on, "Joe, you've simply got to tell us what you've been up to all these years. I heard about the accident. It was so . . ."

"What accident?" Blake touched my arm with his strong brown hand, and one of the many irreverent little gremlins that romp in my psyche made me think: *My god, he's going to heal the cripples.*

"Joe," said Martha, "was on the Olympic downhill team, and . . ."

"And I crashed and burned at Grenoble. But you couldn't call it an accident. I was taking dumb chances." *I was also winning, until the edge caught, but you don't say those things.* So I sipped my wine and grinned just as though that was all water over the dam, just as though I hadn't refought every inch of that race a thousand times a year since it happened, bad enough in daylight and worse in dreams, the unheard scream, the wake-up sweating, Rita scared until she knew why, knew that Joe Bird wasn't in the big brass bed upstairs at Joe's Place but cartwheeling ass-over-teakettle down a well-iced race course on a tall French rock, falling, twisting, screaming because his knee was facing backward. I'd been getting better about the dream lately. It only came about once a month now.

Martha's voice floated across the table: "But you're all right now?"

"Oh, sure. I ski." *And turtles fly.* My right kneecap has been cleverly rebuilt out of nylon and stainless steel, but not quite cleverly enough. I ski, faking it mostly, and even then the leg starts to go after five or six hard runs, and I spend too many hours forcing myself not to think how it used to be, what it could have been. But you don't say those things, either.

"Well, then," said Blake, "it's settled. You've got to show us the hill." He sipped his beer, and the hint of a frown appeared on the patrician forehead. "Neither Martha nor I have ever skied Snowmass."

I looked at him and thought: *Here is a man whose every move is plotted weeks in advance, who has advance men figuring out the best parade routes, aides to brief him on the name of the next guy moving down the receiving line, a whole apparatus that does nothing but focus the energies and the persona of Senator and Mrs. Blake Ross.* He had all that, but not in Aspen. And as I sat there I had the funny feeling that I had just been appointed Blake's advance man in the ski country of Colorado. It was a part I wasn't at all sure I wanted to play.

Then I looked at Martha, and found myself saying, "You'll like Snowmass. Did you get to ski today?"

"Actually," said Martha, "we just got in this afternoon. There was fog."

"We were three hours in Stapleton airport."

Blake's answer drifted past me. I heard their nice conversational words and made nice conversational replies, but inside my head it was nearly twenty years ago and Martha Edwards and I were both seventeen in the springtime, in Eagle Grove, Kansas.

Eagle Grove wasn't a bad town, just very small, and very flat, and very ordinary. It was a town of wide lawns and wide front porches on clapboard houses, porches that some people still called "verandas," and big wineglass elms, dogs and bicycles, three churches, all various kinds of Protestant, one high school, one movie. And Martha's father, Mr. Sam Edwards.

At the far edge of town where the railroad tracks sliced into the distance in permanent, silent invitation, there stood eight enormous gray concrete grain elevators rising like some mythical castle from the plain. "EDWARDS" was painted on each of them in huge blue letters, in case you had any doubts about who owned them, and most of the rest of the town to boot. You could see the Edwards' towers from anywhere on that dead-flat plain: they were the dominant physical fact of our town, just as Sam Edwards was the dominant human factor in Eagle Grove. From the top of those towers you could damn near see Wichita. You could also see, from the top of Sam Edwards' towers, the Edwards Hotel, the Edwards Ford car-truck-tractor dealership, and Edwards'—our one department store. And if you squinted northwest, about ten miles outside of town, you'd see a gentle rise that Mr. Sam liked to think of as a hill. There was a clump of green on the rise, and behind it a flash of white. Those were the trees and that was the main house of the old Edwards farm, where it all started; they lived there still, although the farmhouse wasn't a farmhouse anymore. It was more like the house in *Gone with the Wind* after Mrs. Sam—Martha's mother—got done with it, all white pillars and elegance. Anyway, in Eagle Grove it was as close to elegance as anyone was likely to come.

My dad always said you could hardly spend a dime in Eagle Grove without four cents of it finding its way into the pockets of Mr. Sam Edwards.

Not that anyone minded. The Edwardses were fine people. Anyone would tell you that, even my father. When pressed. After all, wasn't there the Edwards Memorial Hospital, loaded with all the latest equipment? And don't forget the Madeline Edwards Park, right downtown, valuable real estate, too, with its white bandstand and its borders filled with whatever flowers could be persuaded to bloom on the dry, windy plain. But maybe the best evidence of the kind of people the Edwardses were was Martha, who could only have happened in a family like that, in a town like Eagle Grove, Kansas, USA.

Mr. Sam was a hellfire Baptist, but Martha's mother was of the Presbyterian persuasion, which is something altogether different. In any case, between the two of them, Martha got a good dose of religion at a very young age, and a lot of it stuck.

Martha grew up with a sure sense of what was right and what was wrong, and even as a little kid she had the determination and the power to set about turning wrongs into rights with a forcefulness that flabbergasted us kids and made even grown-ups take notice.

I can't recall a time before I knew her.

The first thing you noticed about Martha Edwards was not her good looks, although sure as you're born she's a beauty, small and straight, fragile as some rare old China figurine, but also strong at the same time. What you got from seeing Martha the first time was a feeling. You knew you were in the presence of a personage. Even when we were kids of seven or eight or ten this was true, and it only got truer as we all got older.

Martha Edwards was not just another little rich girl. She was a force of nature.

Wherever Martha was, things happened, and happened fast, and they were good things, things that needed to be done, but somehow only Martha saw it, or cared enough to set about doing it, whether it was feeding a stray dog or helping a family of itinerant harvesters. Even as a kid Martha had this great longing for the future: it couldn't happen soon enough to please Martha Edwards.

And in the meantime, there was so much to do, and only her to do it.

"Mr. Sam," I once heard her say gravely to her daddy, "Mr. Sam, I saw a little girl this afternoon who was shivering, she was that bone cold, and she only had a thin little Easter coat and it didn't even fit right." And a package would arrive from Edwards' Department Store. I recall one time a dog got run over at the intersection of Franklin and Elm streets, just an old dog, a stray, or at least no one claimed it. Not a week later the public-works people came to put a stoplight at Franklin and Elm, Martha's doing, someone told me, although she'd never mention her good deeds herself, not ever.

You couldn't count all the good things Martha caused to happen in that little town. If this makes her sound like a goody-goody, she wasn't. Martha liked her fun, and there was mischief in her as much as any kid. But there was this other thing too, this special sense of caring. We were not a mean bunch of children, but none of us could hold a candle to Martha when it came to being thoughtful, to doing the right thing.

She would have been outstanding anywhere. It was the nature of Eagle Grove, small as it was, closed in as it was, that she stood out that much further.

In Eagle Grove, people came neatly divided into categories: good, better, best. There is no snobbery quite like the snobbery of a very small town. You'd hear tell of so-and-so being Of Good Family. That meant they didn't actually rob or kill. The Better Families included any professional or small businessman and maybe some of the more prosperous farmers. The category of Best was an easy one to learn in Eagle Grove. It consisted of Martha Edwards, her parents, and her dog, Fred. There was another, catch-all, very low category in our cast-iron social structure. It was called Good-for-Nothing, and you hardly ever heard it used. When you did, it was applied against strangers, fallen women, drunken uncles, foreigners, Jews, Catholics, poor people from other places, any kind of deviant, and Democrats.

It would be misleading to suggest I grew up with Martha Edwards, because she was hardly ever there. But since my father was principal of our little high school, we were counted among the Better Families. That is, we could read and write, owned books, were unlikely to pocket the silver, and it was okay for me to mingle with Martha Edwards.

When we were very young, Martha went to the local grammar school.

There was the usual routine of kids' parties, and now and then hayrides and barn dances. Martha would be driven into town every morning in Mr. Sam's big black Lincoln Zephyr that fascinated all the kids because it had a twelve-cylinder engine you could hardly hear and round push buttons set into the sleek doors instead of ordinary door handles like other people's cars. Mr. Sam's car seemed to glide where lesser machines sputtered and lurched. And in the back of that big black car sat Martha, straight and slender, as close to a fairy-tale princess as I had ever seen.

I was quiet as a boy, and more than a little shy. Martha seemed unreal to me, a vistor from some distant, infinitely desirable planet to whose entrance gates only she and her family had the key. She always smiled, with that unselfconscious politeness that was bred into her bones. But we were never anything like close.

Then one day we were seventeen.

To be seventeen and poor in a town like that is a special kind of torture. You know the world isn't flat, no matter what your eyes tell you, searching restlessly across the unbroken plain. And you study that thin line far away where the sky meets the wheatfields the way a condemned man might look at the lock on his cell door, gathering every atom in your body for the moment of escape.

I didn't hate Eagle Grove, but I felt it suffocating me. There were days when it seemed hard to breathe.

I read books some, studied some, and I ran. Running seemed to come naturally to me. Our little high school wasn't much for teams, even though there was an endless supply of huge farmboys for football. But Joe Bird ran.

The running was an escape in itself, because after the first mile or so you find yourself in a kind of a trance, drifting in a special world of your own making, a hyped-up oxygen high the coach said, rightly or wrongly. Whatever it was, I loved it, and running truly became the means of my escape from Eagle Grove. I began winning. I set a few records. I got to run the mile at Wichita, which was as far as I'd ever been from Eagle Grove. And the colleges began scouting me. I was offered four scholarships and chose the University of Colorado at Boulder. Boulder! There would be nothing flat about Boulder. Boulder was escape. I would cross my horizon at last.

I knew it could be done. Martha Edwards was proof it could be done. She crossed and recrossed the far horizon as casually as I walked to the movies. And got prettier every time.

Martha was going to boarding school by then, in Massachusetts.

It's odd how you can know a person on and off for nearly eighteen years before you really see them.

The first time I truly saw Martha Edwards was on a Saturday night early in June, in 1962.

She stood in a white dress next to the big white pillars of her daddy's house on that rise outside of town, welcoming people to the cookout. It was the purple time of day just after sunset. The afterglow was light enough.

Martha gave me a smile big enough for the whole world, and just then I noticed that about a hundred white French lilac trees were in roaring bloom nearby.

"Hi, Martha."

"Joe Bird! I'm so glad to see you."

"How've you been?"

"Just fine, I guess, Joe. How have you been?"

How had I been? I'd been a prisoner, I'd been the Count of Monte Cristo, and now I was free, about to ride off into the sunset in search of my fortune, trailing glory! Will you come with me, Martha? Will you help build my dream? I choked and stammered and managed a smile.

"You look different." That wasn't what knights in shining armor said, but it was the best I had on me.

"Mama says I am absolutely wasting away." She laughed. Bells rang. Heavenly choirs. Fireworks. Victory parades. "It's the food at school."

"I meant, good-different."

"Well, thank you, kind sir. That is a relief. Joe, you must meet my roommate, Susie. I told her what a famous track star you're getting to be, and she's all agog."

"When she begins setting up hurdles, I'm leaving." Not only a track star, Martha, but a great wit. My mind was turning to Wonder Bread, and Martha Edwards was doing it. Do you need anyone killed, Martha? A few bridges burned? Mountains moved? Seas parted? I'm here, Martha, I'll do those things. She went on. She didn't understand. My life was changing right here on Mr. Sam's fancy front porch.

"No," Martha continued, giggling, "you'll like Susan."

I did like Susan well enough, and the rest of the party too, but the next day I couldn't remember Susan's last name. Fact is, I could hardly remember my own.

When they talk about people falling in love, they must mean Joe Bird, age seventeen.

It was more than a fall. I plummeted.

Puppy love, you may say, a passing fancy. That is what I kept hoping. Every night for years.

As romances go, we didn't set any speed records.

All we had was that June, what was left of it, and mostly all we did was talk and laugh and dream. I'd borrow my father's car and drive her to parties. She'd enlist me in her various good works. Or we'd go riding on Mr. Sam's English saddle horses, or shatter clay pigeons by the hundreds on her daddy's private target range. And everything Martha did, she did with a quiet ease: she rode with the fluid grace of poured syrup. She shot deftly, with an eagle's eye. She was a born hostess, a delightful guest. She came to my last high-school track meet, and we won.

But mostly what we did was sit on her big back terrace with a jug of lemonade and talk through the long June afternoons while mile after mile of her daddy's new green wheat rippled out like some edible ocean toward the horizon.

One day I realized that horizon was not my enemy anymore: Joe Bird had tamed the horizon, and one day soon he was going to cross it, and leave it behind, maybe forever.

We talked and we talked. Martha was a fountain of dreams, only for her they weren't exactly dreams. They were realities that hadn't happened yet. Maybe what I loved in her was this soaring lack of limitations. She simply did not acknowledge the word "impossible." And the only times she got anything like angry was when other people seemed slow to share her vision.

"It makes me downright furious, Joe. Just livid!"

I loved her glad, I loved her angry. Either way, her gray eyes sparkled and changed the way an old fire opal my mother owned would change as you turned it in the light. "In New York there are people who don't even have shoes, Joe, let alone enough to eat. And there's just no reason for it, no reason at all." I agreed. I would have agreed if she'd told me the moon was a marshmallow, or if she'd asked me to step right off the top of her daddy's grain elevator, or eat thistles, or fly.

"When I grow up, Joe Bird, do you know what I mean to do?" *I don't, Martha, but whatever it is, please, please, God, do it with me!* I couldn't answer, so she went on: "I am going to go out into the world and change it, really and truly. It can be done."

And there you have a measure of the enormous difference in the level of our expectations. Martha was going to change the world, and all I wanted to do was get out of town.

June went by too fast, a gentle rush of soft green days and quiet blue nights. We went picking watercress in a stream, she laughed and took my hand and the electricity shot through me just as though I'd touched a high-voltage wire. I don't think she noticed a thing.

My summer job began on the fourth of July, lifeguarding at our little local lake, and Mrs. Sam took Martha to France and England for the summer and that was that. Once, the night before she left, I worked up all my courage and kissed her. But it was a brother-and-sister kiss, there was no sex in it. We didn't even have a love song.

Then came college, and we truly lost track of each other, me in Boulder, Martha at Smith. She announced her engagement to Blake Ross on another June night five years later. They say it was a lovely party.

I didn't mind so much, because by then I had another love. Destiny seeks out some people, but I drove up to mine on an old Greyhound bus.

The bus ground relentlessly across the plain from Wichita, running the full ripe tedium of the plains, wheat upon wheat, grain enough to feed the world. Hundreds of miles of wheatfields, and somewhere in the middle of them Joe Bird moved through his old horizon without even batting an eye. Late in the afternoon we crossed the Colorado border. I went back to my book. The Prince of Denmark wanted out, too.

When next I looked up, it was to see the splendid purple wall of the Rocky Mountains rearing up like God's own painted backdrop, towering over the prairie, which turned out not to be endless after all. Maybe nothing is endless.

I loved those mountains at once and forever: they were so much taller than Sam Edwards' eight gray grain elevators.

The look of the mountains was nothing compared to the feel of them rushing under my skis.

The day after the first good snowfall in Boulder, I became an instant ski bum. Oddly, the running helped. I had good wind, a wiry build on a six-foot frame, and endurance. The basics of skiing came easily my first time out on borrowed skis. It wasn't just the speed that got me, or the bumps and the thrill of it.

What I loved about skiing then—and now—was the liberation of it, the feeling of flying, of making the hill work with me the way a hawk works the wind.

All that college year I worked, ate, slept, and breathed only for skiing.

I worked Christmas vacation tending bar for lift tickets, skiing every morning, pouring beer all night. At midterms I nearly lost my scholarship. Reading isn't easy when you're cutting through powder at better than sixty miles an hour.

Sophomore year I made the ski team, and it was a winning team. I was drunk with it. I skied my way into the Nationals, to a long undusted shelf filled with cups and urns and medals, skied my way into a kind of small local Colorado fame and into the beds of many cheerful girls whose names I never got quite straight even then. I skied my way onto the United States Olympic Team, and to an unscheduled rendezvous with a tall French fir tree at Grenoble. And that was that.

"Joe. Joe? Hey there!" Martha put her slim hand on mine. "You always were a dreamer. But how did you happen to settle in Aspen, of all places?"

She really had no idea. *I'm on the lam, Martha, running and hiding where my dreams and my demons can't find me. I thought the mountains would stop them, Martha. I thought I'd never see you again. And I was wrong, wasn't I?* My answer came riding at them on a smile: "Well," I said, easy, chuckling modestly, as befits one who has much to be modest about, "you might say I sort of fell into it. After Grenoble, it was pretty obvious there wouldn't be much future for me as a coach—which is what I'd thought of doing—so I took a little money my grandmother left me and sank it all into this place. Worked my tail off for a few years. But now it's going all right." *It was, anyway, Martha. At least it seemed to be.*

Until about twenty mintues ago when you strolled in here and kicked the shit out of my little red wagon.

"It's a very nice place, Joe." She had a touch of the tone you might use praising a child who's just finished making a specially nice sand castle.

"I'll say," Blake added smoothly, and all of a sudden something made me want to tell them both why Joe Bird was really in Aspen, not just because of Martha, although surely she was part of the reason. I was hiding, on the lam from a lot of things, and while Martha might be the first and foremost, there were others. In fact, there was the whole goddamn world and everything in it. Everything that Senator and the lovely Mrs. Ross were out to patch up and polish and set all bright and shiny in the store window. Well, I'd taken a good look at their world and run like hell. There were no plans in my mind to stagger onto my white horse and change that world. It seemed to me that there was so much dirt and deception and ignorance and hatred out in that wide world that any one person trying to fix it would have about as much effect as trying to bail out the ocean with a thimble.

I didn't like the world's reality, so I tried to make my own.

If it was fenced in on all sides by twelve-thousand-foot mountains, if my imagination and conscience went on automatic pilot beyond the walls of Joe's Place, if I avoided deep human commitments the way a skier avoids crevasses, if I honestly didn't care that much, what harm was I doing except maybe to someone else's concept of what one half-crippled thirty-six-year-old semi-ski-bum named Joe Bird ought to be?

In Aspen I tried to make my own reality, my own peace. The mountains and the skiing helped: big mountains impose a kind of reality of their own, ageless and irrevocable. Aspen itself, Aspen the town, with its skiers and service industry, with its glitter people and artsy-craftsy people, with its glossy look of carefully cultivated health and beauty, its staggeringly high per-capita income, with all this Aspen has evolved from the ghost of a roaring silver boomtown into a very special kind of escape mechanism all its own, with its own pleasures and dangers and traps. Part of the danger is when you begin to believe Aspen is real. I hadn't gone that far yet, but it was easy to see how other people did. I could tell you about several such folks presently rebounding off the walls of their expensive padded cells, and of at least one golden young ski racer who now wears a pine box.

It was getting late. Maybe it was the candlelight, but it seemed to me there was a certain strain about Martha's eyes, a kind of tension. Well. Three hours at the airport: it had been a long day. We talked lightly for maybe half an hour more.

Then Martha said they'd really have to be going, but could we all ski together the next day? They asked me for breakfast, but I put it off, saying we'd all meet later in the morning on the Big Burn, fine, all agreed, and of course I'd stay for supper. Smiles, handshakes, a half-buried yawn, promises: I'll never learn.

2

Rita was already in my big brass bed when I came up from helping Charlie and Rick batten down Joe's Place.

I live on the top two floors over the bar. Charlie and Rick bunk in a room behind the kitchen, and Rita has a room of her own on the second floor, down the hall. Sometimes she uses it and sometimes she doesn't. *Droit de seigneur* is not written into anybody's working papers at Joe's Place. But Aspen nights are long and we had drifted into a warm and easy relationship, part kidding and part almost-serious, no vows exchanged, no contracts signed, no pledges of eternal anything.

Just the way I like it.

Rita had been with me nearly a year on that Thursday night in February, and a year is a very long time for a girl like that in a town like Aspen. But one of the reasons I was in a town like Aspen was not to have to count the days. Or the nights, either.

She put down her paperback edition of the poems of Emily Dickinson. " 'I see him,' " she quoted, " '. . . in the star, and meet his sweet velocity in everything that flies.' " I looked at her, planning a little sweet velocity of my own. She grinned, ever a mind reader. "That," said Rita, "is quite a pair, your pals Mr. and Mrs. Senator." She yawned sexily. Rita did almost everything sexily, and was most of the time totally unaware of the effect. Part of the fun was reminding her.

"Yeah. It wouldn't exactly astound me to find them being Mr. and Mrs. President one of these days." I got out of my boots, hung up what I was wearing, and stepped into the adjoining bathroom to brush my teeth. I could hear her voice floating smoothly and gently over my splashing. Rita is a Boston girl, but she somehow avoided that sandpaper twang. It's a gentle voice, almost southern, and very precise. "You can see," she went on, "that he's running for something."

"Maybe not." I came back into the bedroom and walked to the window to close the shutters against the draft and against the light of dawn. I looked out over the sparse lights of Aspen toward the huge dark-purple bulk of Ajax Mountain looming beyond the town. The snow had stopped but the air held that special quiet that only the insulation of new snow can bring. Across town somewhere a car's engine raced and faded. There was no other sound at all. I closed the shutters and turned to her. "Some people are just like that. Bigger than life. But they are pretty dazzling. I more or less grew up with Martha. We lived in the same little town, anyway. Martha Edwards, she was."

"She has a nice face."

"She's a nice lady."

"You didn't get a feeling he was kind of counting the house?"

"You," I said, sliding into the warm bed next to her, "are too beautiful to be such a cynic, young lady. Blake Ross could be one of the great leaders of our time." I kissed her neck. She giggled and squirmed out of my reach.

"And I," she said through a screen of laughter, "could be the Empress of Japan. You really buy that great-leader crap?"

"I'm not sure. What does a one-eighth Cherokee, half-crippled ski bum know about politics?"

"You're not a ski bum." Her voice was sleepy.

"In my heart I am. And other places. Anyway, you've got to admit it's possible. He could be a great leader."

"Sure." She turned toward me and put her tongue in my ear. "Everything's possible."

"Yeah. Yeah!"

"Joe?"

"Ummmm?"

"Are you really part Cherokee?"

"Not that part. He's all American."

Her laugh filled the bed almost as much as the warmth of her. "Just loves standing at attention." Rita's hand followed her words.

"Right. And here comes the parade."

* * *

Friday dawned blue and glorious over two inches of new powder.

That decided me.

I'd been holding back, thinking maybe I'll make excuses, just not show up, maybe there's some urgent business in Denver, maybe I'll just change my name and flee the country. But one look at that powder, and Martha or no Martha, it was out of my hands.

There are days in Aspen that simply have to be skied.

I dressed without waking Rita, gulped down some juice, and aimed my new green 911S Porsche the ten quick miles west to Snowmass, ignoring the other two perfectly good mountains I passed on the way, one of them—Ajax—growing not five blocks from my doorstep. Snowmass it would be.

About half of last year's profits had gone into the Porsche—my one big luxury. And every time I got behind the wheel the investment justified itself in one swift rush of pleasure and power and the special thrill of handling a car that responds lean and quick as a ski.

I broke my own record to Snowmass.

The general idea is to be the first one on top of the Big Burn.

If you've ever skied the Burn, you know why. It's a dream trail, simple as that, damn near one mile wide, a huge pristine meadow eleven-something thousand feet in the thin mountain air, great loping fields of white dotted with clumps of fairy-tale fir trees, at one point cutting through an entire evergreen forest, the kind of place where you can make your own trail as you go along, maybe taking it easy in a series of big half-mile-wide loops and zigzags to get the last inch of pleasure out of your run; or maybe that time you feel a little show-off and you decide to plunge dramatically through the greenery down the lift line, using the big steel towers as marking poles for your own private slalom course, and down you plunge, maybe yodeling, all speed and angles, spewing plumes of powder as you thread your way between walls of trees and rows of towers, all stops out, showing the tourists how it's done.

It takes three major chair lifts to get to the top of Big Burn—four, if you count the little parking-lot lift at the bottom, which I never use, since I park in the condominium slot of a lady I know, higher up the hill.

There were four people ahead of me going on number-2 lift, but maybe because all the shortcuts on the connecting trails are as familiar to me as Rita's smile, it really was me, Joe Bird, first and triumphant on top of Big Burn that Friday.

I ought to be too old to take pleasure in such things. Fat chance.

I skated off the chair and took the hard right turn that leads into Powderhorn, the long snaking trail that marks the far-left perimeter of the Burn.

The powder that day might have been made from angel's breath. I moved down Powderhorn as if pursued by wolves, all the juices in me churning with the compulsion to be first.

Powderhorn starts off deceptively gentle, cresting along a ridge, cutting a wide lazy swath through stands of giant sentinel firs and then veering dramatically down and down, fast and tricky and seductive, plunging past ten thousand arrow-slim Aspin trees the color of old chinos and then easing off a bit toward the bottom, all in all better than four miles of finest skiing anywhere, gilded with that dust-dry powder over a base that must have been more than forty feet packed hard.

If you're very good and you die they might send you to a trail like Powderhorn on a day like that Friday.

The trouble with being first is that it only happens once a day.

From the bottom of Powderhorn up the number-5 lift takes a good fifteen minutes, after which you ski down a connecting trail to the Burn lift, which takes another fifteen mintues on top of that. By the time I got to the top of the Burn again it was nearly ten o'clock and fairly well-populated. Not crowded: the Burn is simply too damn big and wide and various for that. Hundreds and hundreds of skiers can be on it at any given moment and it'll still seem dead empty.

I skied the lift line and racked up another first. No one else had been there yet that day. The lift line's a bit hairy for most people, steep as it is, and narrow, and punctuated by those very visible but very unyielding steel towers.

There is this almost eerie special pleasure I get, carving my own private signature on virgin snow. It's like your first time with a beautiful girl, and every swoop and turn is transformed into the private voyage of discovery, and the million quick instinctive decisions your body makes faster than your mind take on all the significance of some great fatal moment in high diplomacy or military command.

And if you zig when you should've zagged, forget it, friend, this is the big time and you have just been wiped out. There are very few second chances on a ski trail.

I made one more run down the Burn, taking it easier this time because the right leg had already begun to throb a little, reminding me that I'd taken the first two runs pretty much all-stops-out. I wanted to save something, to be able to look good for Blake and Martha when they showed up. If they showed up.

The senator from Pennsylvania saw me before I saw him.

I skied into the line for the Big Burn chair lift and automatically called out: "*Single*!" the way you do when you're skiing alone, which makes double chair lifts one of the world's better inventions for meeting girls.

"Hey! Joe Bird!"

Blake Ross was standing a little to the side of the line, tall and unmistakable in a blazing yellow parka and dark-blue stretch pants. We paired up and began moving with the line.

"Where's Martha?"

"The secret of our happiness rests on two things, Joe: I promise never to be her bridge partner if she promises never to ski with me. But we're meeting for lunch in that place up there." He gestured with his pole at Sam's Knob Restaurant on the crest above us to the right. "So why don't you join us?"

"Thanks. I'd like that."

The lift line moved forward with that curious silent shuffling of people clamped to skies in limited space on level ground, sliding and maneuvering and usually not saying so much in their single-minded effort to keep that lift line moving just as fast as politeness would allow.

Blake didn't say much either. In the merciless sunlight of just before noon, he looked older than he had the night before. Martha, I knew was exactly my age—thirty six. In this light, maybe after a restless night, maybe because, for all I knew, the cares of the world were on his broad shoulders, Blake looked at least ten years older than that.

As we made our way along the narrow, roped-off path that led to the chair, I got some small indication of what it must be like to be Blake Ross.

People looked at Blake instinctively, because he was a man to stand out in any crowd. Then it would dawn on them who this beautiful stranger was, and they'd start and look again. For movers and doers, there is no such thing as incognito. I counted at least half a dozen comical double-takes in the five or so minutes before we got to the chair.

Well, Blake had sought the limelight, and he wore it well. He moved through clouds of recognition effortlessly, chatting lightly, now adjusting a buckle on his ski boot, laughing, checking his watch, perfectly normal. No. Not perfectly. A little tense. Maybe that's hindsight, but I felt it at the time. Blake simply seemed not to notice the attention he was getting. Maybe a few years of continuous-performance celebrity can build up that kind of immunity in a person. All I know is, it made me squirm, as if I somehow owed the world a performance in a play I'd never read, or rehearsed, or even liked very much.

The Big Burn chair lift grabs you fast and lifts you firmly into the clear Aspen air.

The chairs have a safety-bar-plus-footrest gadget that is up when you sit down in the chair, and swings down over your head to rest on the armrest, creating a thin steel-tube barrier all around you so that you're actually in a kind of cage, a miniature park bench gliding maybe fifty feet in the air with a fantastic sense of quiet and only a very gentle rocking motion that is almost hypnotically soothing, as though all the world were being run in slow motion.

Unless you're talking, the only sound is a low distant hum from the steel cable overhead and a faint clicking when you pass a tower. I love chair lifts. They're very unreal.

The Big Burn chair lift takes fifteen minutes to travel about seven thousand lateral feet.

For the first third of its journey up the mountain, the Big Burn lift runs through a cut in a dense fir forest. Then the forest thins out abruptly to become that famous big wide meadow—the actual "burn" that gives this part of the mountain its name, site of a big forest fire a generation ago that cut a swath not yet healed over. At the top, beyond the meadow, the woods close in again.

Blake and I rode companionably through the thick of the woods, not saying anything of importance, floating above the steepest part of the lift line, where I could still see my own lonely tracks in the snow, curve on sweeping curve. My handwriting should only be that precise, that easy.

I asked Blake how he'd met Martha: no one had told me.

They'd met in Washington, Martha's first year out of college, when she was a volunteer in one of the Kennedy poverty programs in the early sixties. Maybe all I wanted was to see Martha through Blake's eyes. I never got the chance.

The sniper picked his spot just about perfectly.

We'd just passed the thickest part of the woods and our chair was totally in the clear, starting its swing across the first open stretch of meadow. It was just then that someone hidden back in the dense woods, back to the right of the chair, pulled the trigger that ended one of the most promising careers in modern American politics.

I didn't hear a thing.

Blake was in mid-sentence. He shuddered a little—not much—and gripped the steel safety bar very tightly.

Blake had been looking at me, goggles up on the patrician forehead, eager, smiling, saying something about Martha. His expression changed, and it changed in slow motion. Not to a grimace of pain. He looked bewildered, as though he'd just remembered an important phone call and now it was too late to make it. It was too late for a lot of things, but I didn't know that yet.

Blake shuddered and slumped forward a little, the astonished expression still on his face. I thought he was having an attack of some kind, maybe heart. The high altitude affects some people badly that way. He looked at me blankly, not recognizing me, and then a spark of acknowledgment came into his eyes.

"He . . . did it." Blake's words came whistling out as if from a far distance: "O'Leary's right. Tell . . . Martha . . ." Now I could feel the strain of it. I sat there wondering what was wrong. He shuddered again. I put my right arm around his shoulders, afraid that he might slip off the chair. It was only then that I felt the blood.

A woman somewhere behind us began screaming.

The chair lift went gliding on over the blazing white ski trail.

Blake Ross got out one more sentence. "Tell Martha . . . to watch her uncle . . ." He shuddered again and that was it. Behind my chair the screaming stopped. It was very quiet on the Big Burn. I looked at my watch: eleven-fifty-three. There is no way to stop a chair lift when you're sitting on it, halfway up its run. And we had come just about halfway. Seven minutes more. I thought of the woods, dense behind us, of how even I hadn't heard the gun, or seen the killer, of how fast and how far a skier could move in seven minutes, of how many trails branched off below Big Burn. A million thoughts crowded my head as I sat there helpless, holding Blake Ross's cooling body, watching the blood trickle out from between his dead lips, unable to stop it from sheeting down the brave yellow parka, dripping all the way down to the innocent snow of morning.

It seemed like a year before we gained the far woods. The big firs closed around us, and for no good reason I felt safer, less exposed. Finally we approached the unloading platform. I waved, unnecessarily, at the attendant. The lift shuddered to a halt, and for one grisly instant it seemed as though Blake Ross was coming alive in my arms.

The lift operator stepped up to the chair.

"What in God's name . . ."

"It's Senator Ross. Shot. Get the patrol. And . . . wait a minute. Try the state police, too. Whoever shot him is probably halfway down the hill by now." I spoke those words and never remembered speaking. A kind of numbness had come over me, mercifully keeping my mind at least one remove away from reality. The true horror of these last fifteen minutes would be a long while getting through. At the time, it was enough to keep from fainting from the shock of it.

Even now the facts of that day blur as I tell them. Events run into each other and crash, and the memories don't always go obediently back into the little niche where I found them. *But who, who in hell was O'Leary?*

The Snowmass Ski Patrol was right there, efficient as ever.

They have a hut on top of Big Burn, and three patrolmen came right away and took Blake's body off the chair and laid him on one of their aluminum toboggans and covered him with a canvas tarpaulin.

There are no resident policemen in Snowmass.

Someone called the Aspen police, who called the state police, and by that time the patrol had the chair lift moving again, and saw to it that the skiers kept moving as they unloaded.

My skis are short orange Olins. Blake's blood spattered them, and only when I looked down to check my bindings did I see it there, and wipe it off with snow. I stood for a moment, dazed, mindlessly watching the chairs start their silent journey down the mountain, and found myself thinking about who might sit in Blake's chair next time around.

They tied his body to the toboggan, and three patrolmen and I skied with it all the way down Snowmass Mountain. It was a sad little cortege, moving slowly through the bright Aspen noon. No rolls of drums or sad trumpet's wail dignified this first stage of Blake Ross's long journey to his grave. Often, as we passed, skiers would pause, watching, silent. The word spread fast, flew ahead of us down the mountain: Blake Ross is dead.

We brought the body to Pierce's house for privacy and because it was closest: the highest house up the mountain. The crowds and the questions got thicker as we wound our way into the more populous, easier slopes at the bottom of the mountain. I thanked God for the heights of Austin Pierce's ambition, that led him to build his house so high up Snowmass, with its own private access road winding up behind the house itself. He saved us agonies of crowds in the restaurants and parking lots at the bottom of the hill.

Blake Ross lay on an old wooden bench in the huge stone-floored entrance hall of the Pierce house. His tall strong body had gone shapeless under the ski patrol's wrinkled canvas tarp, dwarfed like all of us in that place by the weight of the killing itself and by the unreal height of the cedar walls that leaped up some twenty feet to meet the rough-beamed ceiling.

It was almost like a church.

Four of us stood silent and numb in that enormous space, watching over Blake as if something else, some further horror, might overtake him. The light cut into the shaded room through one tall slit of a window in the paneled wall. The light splashed across the gray stone floor and over the crumpled shape on the bench. But no sun would warm Blake Ross ever again. The hallway was tall enough, and dark enough, and full enough of sadness to be a cathedral. The three patrolmen and I stood there, silent mourners, incongruous in the bright uniforms of skiing, as the snow melted unnoticed off our gaudy boots.

Another patrolman had skied down to tell the police where we were. And they were combing the mountain for Martha. And for the killer, although we all felt the killer must be halfway to Denver by now.

Austin Pierce's big house was staffed by a German woman—a housekeeper-cook—and day help rung in from the village. The housekeeper had gone off to make coffee. And still we all stood there, saying nothing, caught in some invisible web of horror. There just wasn't anything to say.

I don't know how long we stood there, but it seemed very long. Minutes and hours aren't adequate to measure what happened that day.

Then the front door opened and Martha walked in on the arm of another ski patrolman. He was a big man and she looked even smaller than usual beside him. Martha wore a long quilted parka of navy blue over navy-blue stetch pants. Her fine small face had gone dead white, and even the rich dark brown of her hair was hidden beneath a bulky knitted navy-blue cap. She looked like a small lost child, a child already dressed in mourning.

And only then did it sink into the thick skull of Joe Bird that I was going to have to tell her about it all, that I was the only one who really knew Blake's last words, whatever they meant. I looked around the hall. Blake's words were some kind of warning. Maybe a warning about Austin Pierce. I didn't want to think about that, not now, not here in his house. That was police stuff. That was none of my business, or anyone else's. Anyone but Martha. Anyone but the killer.

The truth of it came roaring at me with the hypnotic inevitability of an avalanche: I was in it up to my eyebrows, and I'd be in it until the whole thing was solved. No exit. Dig we must. Damn the torpedoes. The panic began rising in me, overtaking the numbness. It was a close race. I lost.

At first Martha seemed not to see the three of us.

She stood for a moment in the doorway, clutching the patrolman's arm, looking down that long path of sunlight toward her husband's shrouded body on the bench.

Then slowly Martha took her hand from the arm of that big, nervous ski patrolman and moved—also slowly—across the stone floor to Blake, quietly, moving in a stately dream, even her ski boots silent on the cold stones.

"Don't look, Martha." I had to say something, remembering all the blood.

She seemed not to hear my words at all, nor feel the pressure of my hand as I went to her and touched her on the shoulder. Martha stood for a moment next to the bench, quietly, looking down. I took my hand from her shoulder. Then she slowly lifted the corner of the tarpaulin.

Two ski patrolmen quickly looked away.

Martha looked at Blake's head, unmarked but smeared with blood. Someone had closed his eyes. I would never forget the astonished expression they held just before he died. Martha looked, and her lips started moving, maybe a prayer, maybe a curse: no sound came out. Then she gently replaced the tarp and turned to me. I still had my pale blue parka on, and it was splashed with his blood.

I put my arms around her and drew her to me. We stood like that for a moment. I could feel the trembling in her arms, convulsive, a wounded animal. And still she said nothing.

"Martha?" The shuddering in her reminded me of Blake's last convulsions. Maybe I had to reassure myself she was still alive.

"I'm glad you're here, Joe. They said . . ."

"I was with him."

"Oh, no. Joe. How awful for you."

There's Martha for you: her life shot to hell and thinking about other people.

"I'm all right," I lied. "The question is, what can I do for you?" She stepped back a little, back from my arms, and looked around the hallway as if she were seeing it for the first time.

"Police?"

"They're on the way."

"Good." Then she looked at me, blinked twice, saw the patrolmen standing together near the door. Martha tried a smile, only the smile didn't work, she couldn't get it to stay in place right. She spoke, softly but clearly, seeing her duty: "You've all been very kind. Let's not wait just here. Maybe you'd like something to drink?" Martha led us from the hall into Austin Pierce's spectacular living room, all glass and views and huge leather sofas and chairs, old Persian rugs on the wide floorboards and, on the starkly paneled back wall, a matched pair of ancient Japanese screens in faded gold and vivid green, depicting a pine forest and mountains.

The ski patrolmen asked for coffee, but I poured myself a huge bourbon, neat, and a generous cognac for Martha.

"This might help a little," I said, handing it to her. "I'm terribly sorry, Martha." What weak little words they were, backed up against what she was facing. What we all were facing.

"Thanks." She accepted the glass and sipped and made a face, a good little girl taking her medicine. It was only then that she remembered her cap. She pulled it off, shook out her hair, and distractedly brushed back a few vagrant strands that tumbled over her eye. She took another small sip of the cognac and shuddered again.

"He flew," said Martha to no one in particular, "too near the sun."

We sat there uncomfortably for ten more minutes, sipping our drinks, not even trying to make polite conversation, waiting for the police, who we knew must soon arrive. The living room was in shade. The sun was westering now, behind the house. But out beyond the huge plate-glass windows the ski slopes of Snowmass still burned bright with sunshine, dotted with a Christmas-card-perfect collection of colorful, heedless skiers having the time of their lives.

Finally she spoke again, dully. "Excuse me for a minute." Martha got up to leave the room. I rose too.

"Can I do anything?"

"I have to call his parents, Joe. Before anyone else does. They'll be destroyed by this. But, can I ask you something?"

"Anything."

"Can you come back later on? After the police?"

"Of course. You're sure you want to stay here?" I was thinking of Blake's words. Of the ghost of a warning in them. Of when—and if—I ought to tell her. Not now, surely.

"I've got to stay somewhere. Come . . . around seven, would you, Joe. There's no one . . . no one to talk to here."

"I'll be there. Count on it."

"Thanks, Joe." She turned to the ski patrolmen. "And thank you. Very much." Martha walked slowly out of the room, and we sat quietly for a few minutes before Billy Medina and Al Coggin and three state troopers walked in.

Now and then the Porsche earns me a speeding ticket, and once or twice Joe's Place has gotten noisy enough to warrant a visit from the fuzz. But I'd never in my life had any real official business with the cops before. Even if Al Coggin was more friend than cop, it made me feel funny. It was turning out to be that kind of day.

"What happened, Joe?" Al spoke first, looking at me as though he'd seen a ghost.

"I'll ask the questions, Alvin, if you don't mind." This came from Sheriff Billy Medina. And all Al's tales about their not getting along came back to me in a hurry. I have known them both for years. Taken separately, you couldn't ask to meet two nicer guys. But Al resents Billy because Billy's younger, better-educated, and outranks him—and comes from Denver originally. And Billy is bugged by Al because Al is very slow and sure of himself and knows Pitkin County from top to bottom and sideways, and has from boyhood, and isn't doing Billy any favors. Watching the two of them go at it is one of our favorite local sports. It looked like they weren't going to let a little thing like violent death interrupt their vendetta.

The three state policemen weren't introduced. Apparently some decision had already been taken to leave the investigation in the hands of the locals, at least for the moment. I had a feeling, thinking about the Ross legend and the Ross—and

Edwards—connections, that the case wouldn't be in local hands for long.

Billy's voice, which by contrast to Al's voice is city-brisk, cut into my thoughts: "Tell us about it, Joe."

"Near as I can figure," I began, picking out the words with all the precision that was left in me, "there was only one bullet. Although I didn't hear it, and I guess nobody else did either. The killer must have been in the woods, behind us and to the right. We were just clearing that first clump of firs, just getting out into the clear over the Burn, when it came."

"How did you know . . . that it had come?" This was from one of the state troopers. Billy looked at him quickly, as if about to reprimand him the way he'd bullied Al Coggin, then thought better of it.

"The senator stopped what he was saying and . . . sort of shuddered. He looked very surprised, as though he'd been expecting it, but not really expecting it, if you know what I mean. At that time, I didn't know he'd been shot. I thought maybe he was having an attack of some kind. Then I put my right arm around him—I was on the left side of the chair—because he sort of slumped over. That was when I saw the blood. And a woman screamed, I guess in the chair behind us." I paused and sipped the bourbon.

"Yes, that checks out," said Billy, and there was something in his tone that bothered me, a suggestion that maybe a few things Joe Bird said might not check out. "She got to us a few minutes ago. Did you happen to notice the time, Joe?"

"When I looked, it was eleven-fifty-three. But that was a couple of minutes after it happened. Say, eleven-fifty. You could probably locate the exact place by the bloodstains. There was a lot of blood."

"We have some people on that. Joe, did he say anything? Did you have any feeling he knew who did it? You said something about how he seemed to expect it, and not expect it. Just what did you mean by that?" I looked at Billy, and at the eight others in Austin Pierce's big living room: Al Coggin, who was almost a friend, the four ski-patrol guys whom I'd known by sight but not to speak to, and the three state policemen, complete strangers. Quite an audience for Blake's last words. And something made me put the brakes on.

Maybe it was the officious, untrusting note that had crept—not very subtly, either—into Billy's voice during these last few minutes. Maybe it was my sure knowledge that whatever I said in this room would be all over Aspen before sunset. And maybe it was just plain gut stupidity. Anyway, I decided that Blake's last words were the exclusive property of Blake's wife. I'd tell Martha, in detail, this evening. She could do what she saw fit. What Blake had said might mean anything. It might mean nothing at all. And why in the world should I kick up more of a fuss than was sure to be kicked up anyway? So I gave it a full half-second's consideration and fudged the question.

"The senator stopped what he had been saying—which wasn't of any importance—and he just looked at me. He looked surprised, like I said. Then, slowly, as though he were telling a story to a little kid, he said, 'He did it.' There was no indication who this 'he' was, or how the senator knew what 'it' was. But that's what he said, just like that, slowly, disbelieving that it had really happened. Then he said something else, but that was private, that was for his wife. It had nothing to with the shooting."

"How do you know that, Joe?" Billy's voice had gone from officious to something less pleasant.

"It was in confidence, Billy. I don't break confidences, especially from dead men. After I get a chance to tell Martha, maybe she'll want to tell you. Maybe she won't. You'll have to ask her."

"How well did you know Senator Ross?" Billy went on without missing a beat, ever efficient.

"Not well at all. In fact, we met for the first time last night, in Joe's Place. I'm an old friend of Mrs. Ross. We grew up together, back in Kansas." *My life story, by Joe Bird, in twenty-five words or less.* I was getting tired of this, tired of the whole day, of death and questions and whatever little games Billy Medina was playing.

"Where was that, Joe?"

"Little place called Eagle Grove. No one's ever heard of it."

"You were skiing with the senator all morning?"

"No. We had planned to meet, no special time, on Big

Burn. I was going to show them the mountain. I ran into him in the Big Burn chair-lift line just before it happened." I took another drag at the bourbon. It was nearly gone now. The hollow feeling in my gut was not gone. I looked down. The blood on my pale blue parka had dried into an ugly rust-colored smear. The walls were beginning to close in on me. It was time to get my ass out of there, away from death, away from their questions.

"Look," I said, using what was left of my willpower to keep a little politeness in my voice, "I've told you all I know. Do you guys mind if I go back to town and change?" I stood up, since they said nothing. I put the glass down and pointed to the stain on my parka. "Do you need this for anything? It's his blood."

Billy looked to the state police as if for advice. The nameless captain shook his head just slightly: no. "We won't be needing that," Billy said quickly. "And, sure you can go home. But don't leave town, okay?"

"Where would I go?" It's a good question. I ask myself that quite often. "By the way, Mrs. Ross asked me to come back tonight. So I'll be here around seven, if that'll be any help. She doesn't know anyone out here."

"Except," said Billy Medina portentously, looking meaningfully at the splendor of the room, "for Austin Pierce."

"He's not here."

"Wanna bet he will be?"

"I'll see you guys later, okay?"

"See you later, Joe." There was less tension in Billy's voice now, as though he'd overcome some very difficult obstacle. "Take it easy."

"Yeah. Well, so long."

"So long."

I walked out of the living room and into the hall. The wooden bench was empty. My legs carried me right past it, no ghosts reached out to trip me, no lightning struck nor banshees wailed. I opened the front door and stepped out into the cool crystal afternoon air. My skis were stuck in a snowdrift by the door. I'd have to ski down the trail a quarter-mile or so to the parking lot. Before I bent to clamp on my skis, I took the blue parka off and rolled it into a fat strap and tied the thing around my waist. I'd seen enough blood for one day. Then I stepped into the skis and glided off down the trail. Behind me the great stone-and-glass bulk of Pierce's house thrust arrogantly into the slopes of Snowmass. It had always looked monumental.

Now it looked like a tomb.

3

Rita was waiting for me. It was only about three-thirty, but it seemed that years had passed since I'd left her sleeping that morning. Rita always looks good. But I'd forgotten just how good she could look. She took my hand.

"I'm sorry, Joe. Al Coggin called. It's unbelievable. And . . . you were right in the chair?"

"It was quite a day on Snowmass."

I walked right to the bar and poured myself another big bourbon. Usually I don't touch anything stronger than wine or beer. This wasn't a usual day.

I took Rita in one hand and the drink in the other and went upstairs. My bedroom is also a kind of sitting room. There's a small fireplace, a big brown leather couch. I put my glass on the mantelshelf and bent to light the fire. Then I sat down and unbuckled my ski boots. And took a good taste of the smooth, warming bourbon.

"Those fucking bastards."

"Who, Joe? Do they have any idea who did it?"

"No. There's nothing. Not a clue. There could've been a thousand people on that mountain. Naturally, by the time the chair got to the top of the Burn, whoever did it was long gone."

"Did he . . . say anything . . . before . . .?"

I guess that's a natural question. I'd probably ask it myself, if things were different. But I'd been asked one time too many. My first impulse was to snap at her; then I realized where I was, and that this was Rita talking, trying to help. "Nothing that meant anything. But I could tell he wasn't surprised. That he might have been expecting it."

"That poor girl."

"Martha?"

"She must feel terrible."

"I guess he was her whole life." I started to drink the whiskey, then decided I didn't really want it after all. "One thing," I went on, setting down the glass. "It answers your question about Blake Ross being for real. They only kill the real ones."

"Joe . . . can I help? If there's anything . . .?"

"Thanks, honey. No."

She touched my cheek with the back of her hand, the nurse taking the patient's temperature. She paused like that for a second, then turned and walked out of the room.

The fire grew brighter and failed to warm me.

"I'll be around," she said from the hallway. "I'll be right here."

"Yeah. Thanks."

I couldn't see any of Blake's blood on me, but I could feel it. Ten minutes of very hot shower made me feel cleaner, but the numbness was still there, bone-deep, all through me. I set the alarm clock for six and climbed into bed. Then I slammed my eyes shut as though doing that might close the memory of Blake's death out of my mind forever.

Maybe fifteen minutes passed this way. There was a knock on the bedroom door. Which meant it wasn't Rita. Rita didn't have to knock. "Come in." My eyes were still clamped shut. I wasn't sure I'd ever want to open them again. The door opened softly.

"Joe?" It was Rick, one of my two tame ski-bum bartenders.

"What's up?" Still with my eyes closed, like a kid playing games.

"We're sorry about your friend, Joe."

"Thanks. Thank you." He was a nice kid. They were both nice kids.

"And there are two city guys downstairs wanting to see you. Fuzz." He said it categorically, with the quick distant-early-warning system of youth. More fuzz. More questions. Just what the doctor ordered.

"Okay. Give 'em a drink. I'll be down in a minute."

But the two city guys didn't want a drink.

I slid into some jeans and a sweater and pulled a comb through my hair and walked slowly downstairs. Joe's Place was filling up earlier than most Friday evenings. The word had got around. Several people came up to me, including a local newspaper reporter. But I'd already decided what to do about that: strictly no comment. So I waved them all off and made my way to the two strangers who sat in a corner, sticking out from the crowd like goats at a racetrack in their sincere city suits and paperwork-white faces.

"I'm Joe Bird. Can I help you gentlemen?"

Help them to the door was what I wanted to do. Then I thought of Martha, and that maybe these guys would know a way to help her, which was a lot more than I did. So I'd play their game. Whoever they were. Whatever their game was. Looking at the two of them, I was struck by how much we take for granted in Aspen. This is a very physical town. You get used to people who are very competent with their bodies, and to a certain look that goes along with that kind of competence, not beauty maybe, but a combination of health and clean body lines and energy and suntans that adds up to something very like beauty. Hardly ever in Aspen do you see someone who looks like he just slithered out from under a rock. This was one of those rare occasions. I could have done without it.

There was a tall one and a short one.

The tall one wasn't old but he managed to look drawn and cadaverous anyhow. The short one had marshmallow cheeks and pointy-toed shoes my father used to call "brothel-creepers" and small, round, expressionless eyes. His mouth was small, too, a goldfish's mouth. The short one did the talking.

"Gart." He half-rose from the table and put out his fat white hand. For all I knew, "Gart" might have been a greeting in Serbo-Croatian. I guessed it was his name. He continued, "This is Vega." The short man—Gart—half-turned his head to indicate his chum. I nodded. Gart asked if there was someplace private where we could talk. I said there was, and offered them a drink. They shook their heads no with a kind of puppetlike precision that indicated long practice. I could tell this was not going to be a fun conversation. Gart managed to speak. "No thanks," he said, as if barking out a command. "Not on duty." So they were on duty. So they were fuzz. I led them upstairs, pausing on the way to pick up a glass of red wine. They might be on duty. Joe Bird was definitely not.

"Nice place." This came from the tall one—Vega. They had invented an interesting new language, these two: hardly ever did they use verbs.

"Thanks." We were in my bedroom now. The fire was still going. I motioned them onto the sofa and took the wing chair for myself. It was more comfortable. And I was beginning to feel a little put-upon. "Now," I continued, all brisk and businesslike, "you gentlemen are with . . ."

"We didn't say." The tall one fed me that line. The short one wasn't far behind him.

"To set your mind at ease, Mr. Bird," Gart began, in a tone that implied serious doubt that someone like Joe Bird could be trusted with such an object as a mind, "we work for the government." *Sure, I thought. Peru.*

"IRS? FBI? CIA? WPA? Look, gentlemen, I'm pretty tired to be playing games. Either you tell me who you are and what you're after or this conversation ends right now." I picked up the phone and dialed a familiar number. "Is Sheriff Medina there? Well, ask him to call Joe Bird when he gets there, would you? Thanks." I put the phone down.

"Not necessary, Mr. Bird." The short one.

"For all I know, you guys are selling goddamn encyclopedias."

"The organization we work for is . . . very special. You remember the Warren Commission? Well, it was under that commission that we were created. To investigate conspiracies."

"Isn't that what the FBI does? I pay them enough taxes: they should do something."

"We operate in . . . a gray area between Central Intelligence and the federal sector, Mr. Bird. The kind of conspiracy we are interested in is likely to be . . . international."

"You think that's why Ross died?"

"We'd like to know for sure." The short one stood up and went to the shuttered window and opened the shutters. I half-expected to see five Chinese Communists sitting on the window ledge. He cleared his throat in an ominous manner, and went on, "Naturally, the senator's death is being thoroughly investigated through normal channels. You might say that we are investigating the investigation. This is why we need your cooperation, Mr. Bird, and your confidentiality."

Wow. Confidentiality. I thought they buried that one with Watergate. Now that Gart had begun to talk, he was obviously warming to the experience. "You are," he continued, "in a unique position in this case."

Right. Uniquely frightening.

Still he went on, "Your friendship with Mrs. Ross, for example."

"I haven't seen Martha for years."

"So you say."

"And so it damn well is."

"Please! We're all friends here, Mr. Bird."

No we aren't. I have friends, and none of them are anything like you two creeps.

He turned and sat down again. "What we'd like is for you to simply observe. Naturally, you will cooperate with the local investigation. But we would like your opinion of, well, of anything untoward that might be going on."

"And I leave it in the hollow tree? Why don't you guys just tag along? A couple more cops won't even be noticed."

"Your levity is uncalled for, Mr. Bird. After all, a man has been killed. A very influential man." This was not news to me. I could still feel his blood on my hand. "We know," said Gart, rising, "how concerned you must be. To get to the bottom of it all. To see justice done."

To see you gone, buster.

"Well?" I got up, too, and the tall one rose in sync, as though we'd both been pulled by the same string.

"All we ask," said Gart, "is simply your cooperation."

I reached for my wineglass, which I'd forgotten in my anger. I took a drink, set it down, and went to the closet and began pulling out some clothes that were less tattered than what I was wearing. "Look," I said, starting to change as I talked, "I've had a pretty rough day. And I've got to meet someone in a few minutes." Gart went to the window again and looked out. The tall one stared at me impassively as I pulled on old but neat gray flannel trousers and a cashmere turtleneck. I might have been a fish in an aquarium. So might he. "Sure I'll help. If I can. How?"

Anything to get them out of there.

"Simply observe. As I said." Gart turned from the window and did something with his little fish lips that might just possibly have been interpreted as a smile. A very creepy smile. "Tonight, for example," he went on, "when you're with Mrs. Ross . . ."

Son of a bitch.

"How did you know where I'll be?"

"Come, now, Mr. Bird. It's our business to know such things. One of the locals mentioned that fact." He said "locals" about the way you might say "earthworms."

"I'm pretty local myself, Mr. Gart."

"Naturally, naturally. At any rate, even the lady herself might have some sort of a clue, something the senator might have said, some little thing whose importance she might not realize."

"But surely they'll ask her that?"

He repeated himself. It was one of the things he did best. "All we ask, Mr. Bird, is that you observe. Is that asking too much?"

"No. I guess it isn't." All of a sudden it was beginning to seem like everything was too much. These creeps. Blake's death. My date with Martha. The world.

"And," he went on, "from time to time . . ."

"We'll have these fascinating little chats?"

"Your irony is cheap, Mr. Bird. We are only trying to do our job."

Try someplace else. Try someone else.

"Sorry." *But I wasn't sorry.* "What about Medina? What about the state police?"

"Naturally, you'll cooperate fully. Help them in any way you can. Please appreciate that our situation is very sensitive in this case. We can't just move in and take over. Our suspicions may be unfounded. But they also may not be unfounded."

"Just what are your damn suspicions?" I had a right to know. I was the one in that chair lift, not these walking vegetables.

"We'd rather not say. We want no publicity of any kind. This is a matter with national—possibly even international—implications. You understand that." I didn't. I did not understand it at all.

"Where," I asked, "can I reach you if anything comes up?"

"We will be in touch with you. Telephones may not be secure. We can't risk complicating the situation by making our connection with you obvious in any way. We will use a code."

"You have to be kidding. I left my Captain Midnight decoder ring back in Kansas."

"You may laugh, Mr. Bird." Gart's mouth quivered in what he may have thought was a smile. "But three times at least, my life has been saved by such code words. We must establish—instantly—who we are, for your security, and we must be able to identify you for our own security. A code is the simplest way of doing that."

"Okay."

If you'll tell me some word that is ingrained in your memory, but something that wouldn't come up accidentally in someone else's conversation?"

"Powderhorn."

"What is Powderhorn?"

"The name of my favorite ski trail on Snowmass."

"No good. Surely people here talk of ski trails?"

He was right, of course. Damn him.

"How about 'grain elevators'?"

"That's better. Yes. That'll do nicely. When you get a message about 'grain elevators,' you will know where it comes from."

Wonderful.

"Sure. Now: can I buy you a drink?" I hoped they'd refuse. I didn't want their lips on my glasses. What they had might be contagious.

"Thank you, no. We have a busy night."

"Then if you'll excuse me, I'll be moving on."

"You're excused."

That little bastard made me feel that I truly had been excused. From my own damn bedroom in my own house. I showed the happiness boys to the stairs and sat down again, sipping my wine, trying to think what I could possibly say to Martha that could reach across the gulf of pain and horror that had opened underneath her this day. Then I went downstairs and told Rita where she could contact me, and slid into my old sheepskin coat and pushed my way through a crowd of questions to the door.

The questions were probably well-meant, but I didn't have the answers, or the time or the patience.

The door to Joe's Place swung shut behind me. For a moment I just stood there in the street and watched the astonishing purple Aspen night sky drag a blanket of silence, embroidered with stars, over my little town. My town. Death's town. Ajax Mountain rose up beyond the edge of Aspen, towering over the valley like some great stone tidal wave frozen forever just at the moment of cresting.

Old Ajax had been just like that for a million years gone by, and she'll be like that for a million more, shrugging off all the feeble scratchings of man and beast, of silver-lode miners and skiers and murderers. The tallest man isn't one inch high in these mountains. They have a way of putting things in perspective. They usually have a way of putting my demons to rest. Not this day. Not this night.

4

You have to be looking for the little back road that leads up behind Austin Pierce's house. It winds up through fir woods and a grove of aspens and ends in a big oval car park that might hold a dozen vehicles. Mine was the only car in sight, so I pulled right up to the back door.

There's a big brass knocker in the shape of a mean-looking eagle sitting on a shield. Maybe the eagle was giving birth to the shield. I knocked. The door was opened almost at once by a state trooper. He was new to me: not one of the three from this afternoon. I told him who I was, and he led me into the living room.

At first I didn't see her.

Martha was sitting low in the big brown leather sofa before the fire, a tiny shape in the enormous room. She wore a long robe of dark red velvet cut with a simple round neck and decorated with small round gold buttons to the floor. The trooper spoke her name, and mine, and Martha stood up and came to me. She put out both her small hands and took my hands. Martha's hands were cold, tiny and fine-boned. I covered them with my own much bigger, browner, cruder hands, and the helplessness I'd been feeling all day came welling up in me like a sudden sickness. There was so much I wanted to do for her, and so tragically little that I or anyone else could do.

She spoke first. "Well, Joe. How are you bearing up?"

You could always count on Martha Edwards, I should have known that. She might be tied to fate's own railroad tracks with the express due any minute, and she'd be thinking of ways to help someone else.

"I have this terrible feeling I'll live," I said, knowing as the words came out that they were the wrong words, that the last thing she needed was wisecracks from a small-time ski bum who probably came off like a finalist in the Tinsel Gallantry awards. My words hung there, cheapening the air between us, waiting for someone to take the curse off them.

Martha tried her best. "Exactly," she said quietly, leading me to the sofa. "Maybe the worst part is being alive when he isn't. Make yourself a drink, Joe. I have a Coke already." She gestured toward the bar. I poured myself a generous amount of Austin Pierce's sourmash bourbon and sat down.

A well-made fire was burning energetically in a hearth so big it dwarfed six-foot logs. A board of cheeses and biscuits lay invitingly on the big round coffee table that was actually a cross section of a redwood trunk. The room was nearly dark but for the firelight.

On any other night I might have given a lot to be alone in that room with that lady. All afternoon, and all the way out to Snowmass in the car, I'd tried to think of the right things to say, the right things to do. And all the things I thought of seemed wrong. I wondered what she'd do now, how she'd fill the rest of her life. "Do you," I asked, "have any kids?" A kid would help, maybe. Part of Blake living on in spite of everything.

"One little boy who died."

"I'm sorry."

"It was better, Joe. The poor little thing would have been terribly deformed. He only lived two days."

So all that was left of Blake Ross was the memory of hope. He had been nearing the end of his first term in the Senate. Somehow in those short years Blake had crystallized all the aspirations of the liberal wing of the Democratic party. It wasn't so much any specific thing that the man had done, or said, but rather what he was as a person, what he stood for. And what he stood for was a sort of unspoken pledge of decency. Here was a man who would always do the right thing, not as a matter of choice or preference, but because it would be impossible for him to even consider the alternative. Here was a man who seemed to exist beyond compromise, above patronage, a fresh clean presence with the brains and charm and energy to inspire a nation and maybe the world. And now all that was gone, utterly and completely.

It was more than the death of a man.

Martha looked at me and smiled a small tentative smile. "Last night," she said, "when Blake and I walked into your bar, it came as a kind of shock to me, Joe, seeing you all of a sudden like that."

Maybe she did remember.

"I was pretty surprised myself."

"It just all came back, you know, the times in old Eagle Grove when we were kids. Somehow I never thought about that all in one piece. I guess I don't think much about Eagle Grove these days."

I don't either. It hurts too much.

"Mostly," she went on, "what I recall is the springtime, those beautiful soft springtimes. Everything in those days seemed to happen on some late afternoon in springtime, all green and soft and . . ."

"And with lilacs."

"Yes! Mom's white lilacs. Are there lilacs in Aspen, Joe?"

"I don't think so."

"Everything was so shiny and hopeful then, and it all went by so fast."

"You were going to change the world."

She stood up then, and walked to the huge window and looked out at the moonlight playing on the deserted slopes of Snowmass. When she spoke, it was as much to herself, or maybe to her dead husband, as to me. "Oh, Blake," she said, "what dreams we had."

"Maybe some of them can still come true, Martha."

Martha turned quickly, as if I'd hit her. For just an instant she looked almost angry. Then she shook her head with an odd jerky motion like a dog shaking off water, as though this might make the pain go away. Then she managed a smile. I thought, looking at her, that it must have been a very expensive smile. She had to reach down a long way to bring up that smile, down past a ton of hurt and horror. She then walked slowly back to the big sofa and stood looking at me from across the lacquered redwood table. She had control of herself now, but there was a catch in her voice when she spoke.

"When you left this afternoon, I cried for an hour, Joe. It wouldn't stop, floods and floods. Then it did stop. I've been on and off the phone ever since. There are so many people to think of, so much to organize—that has to be done right. It isn't like an ordinary death."

"He was much more than an ordinary man."

"Thank you. He was that."

"Will the funeral be in Washington?"

"No." She sat down and sipped the Coke. "There will be a memorial service in Washington, then a funeral train to Philadelphia, then a private service. Family burial."

"Martha, if I can help at all, just ask. If you'd like me to be there . . ."

"Thanks, Joe. You are helping, right now. Just by being here. But it will be all right. As all right as it's ever going to be. I fear for his parents. They'll just be destroyed by this. He was their whole world. As he was mine."

Somewhere in the house a telephone rang.

"God, but I hate that machine," she said. "It has no mercy. I spoke to Uncle Austin. He'll be in tomorrow. And he's doing things, sweet man that he is, coordinating with Blake's staff, all that."

"It must be complicated."

"I mean to keep it as simple as possible, the funeral." She turned to look at me. "Blake made his life belong to the world. I think his death belongs to me. Is that selfish, Joe?"

"I think it's absolutely natural."

"Thank you. I may have to fight for it. And I'm not sure how much fight there is left in me."

I was. There always had been and always would be more fight in that woman than a regiment of marines.

"You," I said, "will be just fine."

"I hope so."

Now was the time, if there was ever going to be a time, for me to tell her what Blake had said in those last awful minutes before he died. I wondered why she hadn't asked. There were some questions I wanted answers to myself, and I wasn't sure how to ask them. Being me, I plunged right in with my boots on.

"Does the name O'Leary mean anything to you?"

She looked at me for a beat or two as though I'd been speaking in Urdu. Then her eyes focused and she gave a short, impatient movement of her head, as if to clear it.

"There was a young man on Blake's . . . I forget what

committee . . . sort of an aide of some kind. Bob O'Leary. I met him a few times, but he isn't all that memorable. Young—under thirty. Brown hair. And he had a kind of crazy theory. At least, we thought it was crazy."

"What was the theory?"

"Well, it had to do with the Kennedy killings. You know how some people, people who are perfectly sane on other subjects, get wacky about that. Bob O'Leary was one of them. He thought in terms of conspiracies, plots, the classic paranoid point of view."

"And he thought this might somehow affect Blake?"

"Yes. Yes, he did."

I could see the doubt, or maybe the fear coagulating in her eyes, clouding her light voice. Because maybe O'Leary was right.

"You see," she went on unnecessarily, "a lot of people equated Blake with the Kennedy brothers. Not only for what Blake believed in, but because of the . . . because of what he projected. And the Ross/Tilden Energy Bill was the kind of thing people like O'Leary thought might trigger . . . But it's preposterous."

Even I had heard of the Ross/Tilden bill. It was making a lot of very big oil people very angry. Angry enough to kill? I found myself wondering exactly how deeply Uncle Austin was involved with big oil. But, hell, Blake was staying with Pierce, after all. If Blake had thought there was a grain of fact in O'Leary's theories, surely he'd have put as much distance—and protection—as he could between Pierce and himself. Or would he? Maybe he'd want to get inside of the situation. But one look at Martha's face told me this was not the time or the place to begin my cross-examination.

"Martha, if this is going to upset you, just kick me the hell out of here. But before he died, Blake mentioned something to do with an O'Leary. What he said was: 'O'Leary's right.' Then he said for me to tell you . . ."

"Tell me what?" She leaned toward me, tense as taut wire.

" . . . to watch Uncle Austin."

"And that was all?"

"Yes."

"That is the strangest thing I ever heard. What do you think he meant?"

"Well, it sounded like a kind of warning."

"Against Uncle Austin? Well, Joe, I realize you don't know the man, but that is like being warned off Santa Claus. Uncle Austin wouldn't hurt a flea, let alone me. Or Blake. Maybe he meant watch out *for* Uncle Austin, that someone might try to harm Uncle Austin. That could be, couldn't it?"

"It could be."

It could be. But it wasn't. And there looked to be no way at all to convince Martha of that. She was a highly unconvinceable lady once she got her mind made up. And no dying words, even of her own husband, were going to erase thirty-something years' worth of affection Martha had piled up for Uncle Austin. Hers was the kind of loyalty that went smiling to the gallows rather than betray a friendship. Well, I'd delivered Blake's message. That should have cleared my conscience. It did nothing of the sort. I could feel the menace in Blake's words even if Martha couldn't. And I could feel the urge to do something about those words—anything—because they kept coming at me and at me like one kamikaze mosquito in a dark summer bedroom.

"How would you feel about my telling the police?"

"Well, Joe, you must do what you think right. But that is a very confusing message. I would dread to see Uncle Austin mixed up in any investigation unnecessarily. I mean, he is a man of some position."

"I won't say a thing. It's between you and Blake."

"We can't bring him back, Joe. I guess I just want to keep the rest of it as tidy as possible."

My glass was nearly empty. Tidy, she said. There is nothing tidy about a murderer's bullet. But I guess Martha knew that as well as I did. She was in shock, still, and maybe she would remain in shock for some time. My job was to make her life easier. If not telling the cops would help her, the cops would not be told, then or ever. And there was always the chance she was right. Blake's damn message was confusing. I wondered if there was a way to find out who O'Leary was, and what his theory had been, without doing something untidy. Well. I'd sleep on it.

Martha put her hand on mine. Her hand was warmer now. "It means a great deal to me, Joe, just to have you here. Someone who really knows me."

"You're going to be fine."

"That is what they always tell the patient just before surgery."

"What'll you do . . . afterwards?"

"I'm not sure, Joe. I almost don't have a home anymore. Not Eagle Grove, surely. We're renting in Georgetown. And I wouldn't want to live in Washington alone, in any case. Maybe Philadelphia. Possibly. I really have no idea."

"Maybe you should go someplace completely new." And far away, Martha, very far away. It was slowly sinking into my alleged brain that she was free now. However gruesome the circumstances. And her freedom was a great big threat to the defenses I'd been building so carefully all these years. My right knee began throbbing. I realized how bone-tired I was, how much more tired she must be.

"I've half a mind to come back here. May have to anyway, for the inquest."

Don't, Martha. Go someplace far, far away. Marry a king, a prince, a president. Don't invade my little town, my little world.

"You have to think about your own safety."

"Oh!" It came out as half a laugh, half a sob. "Oh, don't worry about that, Joe Bird. They never kill the wives."

"You don't have any idea at all who might . . .?"

"None. There are the usual loonies, who write and phone any public figure, but you quickly learn not to take them seriously. We always knew there was the potential for . . . this kind of thing. It's part of every politician's nightmares. And the better the man, the more likely it is. After a while you get to not thinking about it too much. Because if you did, Joe, you'd go bonkers."

"I see that."

Martha stretched her slim neck back until her head was resting on the low back of the overstuffed leather sofa. She stayed like that for a minute, looking up at the beamed ceiling twenty feet above. Then she closed her eyes. The only sound came from the big fireplace. A log hissed like an angry cat.

When her voice came, it was soft, the memory of a voice from another time, from another place. "At least," she said, "he died before they could make him dirty. Before they could drag him through the filth, and question his dreams too closely. He died intact, with his vision clear."

I watched her, fascinated.

"We need heroes," I said, wishing to the bottom of my socks that I meant it.

Martha opened her eyes then, and turned her head to look at me. She smiled. "*I* sure do. And heroes die young. Or maybe it just seems that way."

I stood up to make myself another drink.

"Could you eat anything, Joe?"

"I don't think so, thanks." I'd had just juice for breakfast and no lunch and no supper. But the thought of swallowing food curdled my gut.

"I can't, either. I had some tea earlier on."

"You ought to have something."

There was another pause. They were getting longer.

Then she spoke. "Joe, have you ever seen a house, or a work of art, or anything that had been vandalized?"

"I don't think so. No."

"We did, once, on Long Island. It was an old beautiful mansion that had just been sealed up with all its beautiful furnishings inside. The owners lived overseas. Well, it was on a big property, and they didn't guard it too well, and after a time people got inside that house and stole things. Almost everything movable, in fact. Well, maybe you can understand the stealing, I mean, if they were poor and all. But they didn't stop at just stealing, Joe. They had to destroy. I remember a beautiful garden room with lots of windows—all broken, of course—and these lovely frescoes painted right in the walls, all vines and flowers and things. Well, these vandals had gone to all the trouble to bring in ugly black paint and deface those murals, write nasty words over them. Not so much on the other walls of the house: just where the most beauty was. And there were other things—awful things they'd done. It was a kind of rape. Whoever did that knew what beauty is. And hated it. Actually sought out that beauty and went to a lot of trouble to make sure it wasn't beautiful anymore. I cried when I saw that house, Joe. It was years ago, but I'd never known there were people like that."

"And somebody vandalized Blake?"

"Yes. People like Blake represent something intolerable to

the vandals in this world. Not power or money exactly, but the fact of standing for something, of giving life to an ideal."

"You don't know of any political enemies he might have had?"

"Not that would kill. No. We had many a fight, naturally, Joe. But they were good, clean fights. Among mostly honorable people. No. None of them would be killers. This has to be a crazy person—like the boy who shot George Wallace."

It was obviously comforting for her to think that. And, God knows, I wasn't coming up with any alternate kinds of theories. But something was wrong about the crazy-assassin idea. In a crowd at a rally, sure. But carefully planted high on Snowmass Mountain on the first skiing day of Blake Ross's not very well-publicized holiday—that smacked of planning, and sophistication, and an organization. It presupposed a crack-shot killer who was also good on skis. Not your usual little seedy neighborhood fanatic. Well, to hell with it. There were more than enough cops of all varieties working on the case, including my own private creeps of this afternoon. I swirled the warming amber bourbon in its glass and decided to call it a night. I could find out more about O'Leary and his wild theories in the morning.

"Well," I said, "one thing we can be sure of is that plenty of good people are looking into it. Martha, who's in this house besides the trooper and the cook?"

"The cook's husband. He's a handyman. But don't worry, Joe. Truly, I'll be fine. I think maybe we both should get some sleep. And Uncle Austin's coming in first thing tomorrow."

"You're sure you're okay?"

"This afternoon was pretty bad, Joe. But I'm in control now. Don't worry."

"Then I'll be shoving off. Call me tomorrow."

"I'll do that. And, Joe: I appreciate you coming out here."

"Thanks."

I stood up, and she followed me out of the room. The trooper was sitting in the big front hall, sitting on the bench where Blake had been laid out, reading a paperback. He stood as we came into the hall.

"Everything all right, Mrs. Ross?"

"Everything's fine, Sergeant. Mr. Bird is just leaving."

I pulled on my big old sheepskin coat—my Abominable Snowman coat, Rita likes to call it—and looked at Martha standing straight and small and defenseless in the big hallway. The hall ran right through the house to the car-park entrance. I was worried about her, trooper or not.

"I wish . . ."

"I know. But really, Joe, I'll be fine. Now, you get a good night's sleep and call me in the morning, hear?"

Typical Martha. Looking out for everyone else.

"I'll do that."

"Thank you for coming, Joe. It meant a lot." She stood on tiptoe and gave me a kiss on the cheek. It burned.

"Sleep well, Martha."

"Good night, Joe. God bless."

I walked out into the quiet night.

There was a half-moon out, and an Aspen half-moon is brighter than full moons I've seen other places. The light was bright and blue at the same time, and it was easy to imagine that it might look like this to be trapped inside a sapphire. The back door of the house opened right onto the car park, and my Porsche was still the only vehicle around. The oval car park was ringed by low pines that gave back onto the fir grove looming black against the clear night sky. Behind the firs you could catch an occasional glimpse of the ski trails threading silvery white among the evergreen black. The quiet was so thick it became a physical presence in the lonely night.

I walked around the car and reached in my pocket for the keys.

It was then that I heard the noise.

It was a faint swishing sound; it could have been an evergreen branch moving in the wind. Only there was no wind.

For no logical reason I hit the dirt, threw myself flat on the driveway, and in the same motion rolled around behind the Porsche. There was a loud metallic "thunk!" as something hit the side of the car. I began yelling: "Officer!"

The door opened instantly and the car park flooded with light. The trooper started out, and I told him to get back, then ran in a crouch to the safety of the house. If it was safe.

Martha stood in the hallway, just behind the trooper, paler than before.

"Joe! What happened?"

"I'm not sure, but I think someone took a shot at me. Except I didn't hear a gun."

"He might have a silencer." This was from the trooper, who motioned us to stand against the wall, out of any possible line of fire. Then he went to the phone, and luckily it worked. I wondered what we'd have done if they had cut the phone lines. Isolated as the house was, it was ideal as a target, perfect for a siege. We could hear the trooper asking for reinforcements. We stood there in the hall, nervously for almost five minutes. Then a big state-police Ford came screaming up the driveway, sirens wailing, lights flashing. There were three troopers inside, and they got out with drawn revolvers, gathered around my car, looked into the woods, then knocked on Austin Pierce's big brass eagle.

"Look at this," one of them said, motioning me to come out.

The arrow had gone right through the sheet metal of my car at just about heart height. It was no wonder. The arrow was the biggest kind of brass-tipped hunting missile, two feet long and capable of stopping a charging bear.

Or a ski bum who heard one last word too many.

There are a lot of bow hunters in Aspen. It's considered more sporting. Our own particular Robin Hood had been hiding behind the low pines, on skis, and we could see where he'd come and see where he'd gone: off down the ski trail, probably before the phone call had been made.

There is no way to trace a ski track.

We had a short war conference inside, and the state-police captain—Richards—managed to yank the arrow out of my car. It was a long, wicked-looking thing with a special deer point that featured three sharp little fins set along the back of the arrowhead almost like a harpoon. The better to cut and shred and make you bleed. That arrow had been scientifically designed to finish off three-hundred-pound buck deer, or even bigger game. It would have been more than adequate for Joe Bird. I looked at it and then looked away.

It was fast dawning on me that now I was no longer a spectator at Blake Ross's murder. I was in it now, up to my ears in it, maybe over my head. Now they were after me, too, and I didn't even know who they were or why they wanted me dead.

I looked at Martha, and thought about my promise not to mention Blake's last warning. If it was a warning.

"Someone," I said slowly, clearly, so that Martha and all four state troopers would hear every word, "someone must think I know something I don't know. Could that be, Martha?"

She got the message.

"Maybe you're right, Joe. Maybe they think Blake said something . . . before he died. I only wish he had."

"I do too. It seems a little superfluous to be knocked off for the wrong reason."

"Joe!" Her face was drawn. I could have bitten my tongue off. She was scared enough already.

"I'm sorry. The irony of it all began getting to me: you know, here I am, Mr. Unpolitical, all wrapped up in something like this."

"Poor Joe." Martha spoke very softly, hesitantly, as though someone unreliable might be listening. As well they might be. I looked at the state cops, and they all looked like . . . state cops. Big deal. Except someone, somehow, wasn't what he seemed. Someone who knew I was coming out to sec Martha. Someonc with the imagination and killing skills to set up the archer in the underbrush. Someone who had a very good idea that Joe Bird knew more than he was saying. Someone relentless.

"What, exactly," I asked Richards, their captain, "would you suggest we do to prevent an encore?"

Captain Richaids was quick to answer. "We'll have to ask you to leave your car where it is until daylight, so we can get a certified trajectory. It's a little stupid—we can see where the guy was—but they like to have it all wrapped up. We can drive you back to town, or maybe it'd be easier for you to stay here."

"Please do that, Joe." Martha's voice was eager, concerned. "We have all kinds of room, and I'd feel better if you did."

"Sure." So that was that. I called Rita and told her what happened, where I was and why, knowing as I spoke that she'd worry, wondering before the words were out if Joe's Place would be next, imagining fires and bombs and who knew what. The game was getting rough, and I hadn't wanted to play even in the beginning.

Martha put me in a guestroom on the second floor, a big room with its own bath. The police assured me the house would be thoroughly staked out all night and that they'd get me a bodyguard in the morning. Wonderful. By this time I was imagining killers wiggling up the drainpipes, but I tried not to let that show. Austin Pierce kept a linen closet well-supplied with extra toothbrushes and spare razors. Martha insisted on fixing me up herself with towels and toilet things and walked me to my bedroom door.

"I don't know what to say, Joe."

What can you say about one sudden killing and a very good try at another? On my best day, with a tail wind, I am far from talkative. This night had me pretty near speechless, and for reasons that went much further back than the flight of that arrow. I reached out in the shadowy hall and touched her arm.

"They're being stupid, Martha, and all that means is, the stupider they get, the sooner they get caught. Sleep well. Tomorrow will be better."

I didn't believe a word of it. I wondered if she did. Martha smiled a small thin smile, said nothing, just nodded, and disappeared down the hall. It was tough to imagine what bottomless terrors she might be taking with her to her lonely bed. I stood in my doorway watching her progress down the hall. A slim, very straight-backed little shape with her head high, brave as hell and probably more scared for me than for herself. I looked at that lady, and it struck my heart with an arrow's quick violent thrust that there was no way at all I could comfort her, not with words, not with love, there was nothing at all to do except get to the bottom of this menace, and fast, and all alone, if that was the way it had to be.

Oddly enough, I slept well that night.

5

I could feel the sun before its brightness woke me. Saturday in Aspen: a busy day for Joe's Place. I wondered if the new shipment of wine would be in today, wondered if the guy would get there to fix the leaky gasket in the kitchen sink, reviewed a dozen other small details in the comfort of Austin Pierce's bed before yesterday's realities cut my everyday existence off at the knees.

Saturday in Aspen. But this Saturday someone might be planning to make it Joe Bird's last Saturday anywhere. It would be a day filled with fear and bodyguards, a day in which I'd have to look at dozens of people I know well and wonder if one of them had the gun, the bomb, the plan, the secret.

The bright morning sun warmed me. I rolled over in the empty bed and pulled the big down-filled coverlet over my head to shut out the sun, the world, my own building dread.

That lasted about half a minute.

Then I got up and made for the shower. I showered and shaved and dressed and went downstairs. Martha was dressed too, in tan slacks and a matching silk shirt and a dark-blue sweater. She looked like several million dollars' worth of widow.

"Good morning," she said, smiling, looking rested. "They're just making breakfast."

"I'm finally hungry." I was, too. Very hungry. We ate in a small breakfast room that faced into the fir woods. The same fir woods that hid the bow-and-arrow man last night. The woods looked soft and peaceful, bright with sun, soft with their deep carpet of snow. They looked like fairy-tale woods, enchanted, as though nothing bad could ever happen there. They lied.

We ate the bountiful breakfast almost in silence. I could see she was hungry, and it did me good to watch her eat. Martha had already talked to the state troopers: no new developments.

After fifteen or so minutes we heard a commotion outside. She put down her fork. The door flew open, and Austin Pierce stood there, all concern and conversation.

"Where is my baby? Where's Miss Martha?" He strode into the little dining room as if he owned it, which of course he did. But there was an unmistakable air of proprietorship about the man; he radiated control. Pierce is one of those men who look about the same from forty to eighty: plump but not fat, neither short nor tall, very well-groomed, a scholar's balding dome with a neat fringe of gray hair, bright blue eyes behind old-fashioned-looking gold-wire-rimmed glasses. Martha shot up and kissed him.

"Uncle Austin!"

"You poor child. Oh, Martha honey, I am terrbily, terribly sorry this had to happen. But don't worry, child. It's all going to be all right now your Uncle Austin's here."

He was wrong, of course. It wasn't going to be all right, ever again. But the man spoke his lines with conviction. I could easily imagine, on some other day, on some other subject, being completely persuaded. I watched him hug Martha Ross, and heard his cheerful words, and thought of Blake, and Blake's warm blood spilling down through the slats of the chair lift onto the snow.

Well, Blake. You asked me to watch the man. I'm watching.

I wondered if Martha was watching him too.

Austin Pierce continued, "You poor child. Tell me all about it."

"Uncle Austin, it just gets worse and worse. Last night they tried to kill Joe Bird."

"Who?" Austin Pierce looked at me for the first time. I stood up.

"I'm Joe Bird, Mr. Pierce."

"Of course," he said, reaching out to shake my hand while still holding Martha in his other hand. "We've met, I believe. Nice to see you. But what's all this? Who tried to kill you?"

I told him what little I knew.

"Shocking. Unthinkable, and in my own driveway. It is possible to imagine why some madman might want to murder Blake Ross. But this—this is incredible."

At that moment Captain Richards came in. Pierce turned to him. "Captain, what do you make of it?"

"One thing's for sure, Mr. Pierce. It won't happen again. From now on we'll have this house completely staked out, and Joe Bird's place too."

Very interesting. Pierce got to be "Mr. Pierce" and I remained old Joe Bird. Status was rearing its ugly head in my informal little town. I wondered exactly how much better grade of protection would be offered to Mr. Pierce than we ski bums rated. Maybe they had a slide rule, depending on how much tax you paid. Unfortunately, the killers didn't seem to care about these little refinements in diplomacy. The killers seemed prepared to be very democratic indeed. I began to feel the Pierce house closing in on me.

"Thank you, Captain," said Pierce, pouring himself a cup of coffee. "I hope this won't distract valuable men from the mainstream of the investigation."

"We've got plenty of help."

"That's good to know." Pierce sipped his coffee and looked at me appraisingly. The blue eyes gleamed coldly through the polished lenses of his eyeglasses. "The trouble with most of these criminal types," he said authoritatively, "is that they're so stupid. Obviously, Joe, they think they have to shut you up. Completely ignoring the fact that you have had a full twenty-four hours to tell the authorities everything you know. It's just beyond belief."

It's just beyond belief until you take a close look at what that hunting arrow did to the side of my Porsche. Until you take a look at what someone's bullet did to Blake Ross. Then, brother Austin, you believe.

"I think," he went on, "that we must be dealing with fanatics."

"Oh, Uncle Austin, don't even say that. I'm really quite thoroughly scared as it is." Martha's coffeecup rattled unmusically against its saucer.

"I am sorry, honey, I got carried away. And after all you've been through." He patted her hand.

"Joe's been just wonderful to me, Uncle Austin. And, really, he is the one who's been through things. He was on that chair lift when—"

"I know, darling, I know. Mr. Bird has been very brave. But let's not dwell on things that may upset you, Martha. There is a lot to be done, and you must save your strength. Everything's arranged. I've got an Air Force jet at Denver, and my own little plane will be at our service here. Naturally. The memorial service is set for Tuesday, then we proceed by car—not train, too public—to Philadelphia. There won't have to be any speeches or interviews or any of that."

She looked at him, nodding faintly as he outlined the plans, and she had the vulnerable expression of a small child being told to wear its overshoes in the rain. I wondered how Martha was going to get through the funeral, and how she was going to get through the rest of her life.

"You," she said, smiling faintly, "are wonderful, as always. But frankly, it's Joe here I'm concerned about. I mean, he only met Blake for the first time on Thursday night, and now . . . all this . . ."

"Damned right, it's terrible." Austin Pierce turned to me with the righteous air of a man who will simply not tolerate terrible things happening around him. "And if there's anything at all we can do, Joe, just let us know."

I wondered if it was typical of Washington power circles to talk of "we" and "us" when what Pierce presumably meant was "me" and "I." Or maybe there was "we." Maybe he had a whole organization behind him. I thought of Blake and wondered, if that was the case, what kind of an organization it might be. And where they did their target practice. He kept right on talking.

"We'll never be able to repay your kindness to this little lady."

"Thank you, Mr. Pierce. I'll be fine. The state police are giving me a full-time bodyguard until this is all cleared up. So please don't worry." I stood up to leave.

"Well, Joe," he said, shaking my hand again, "take care. We'll be in touch."

Don't hold your breath, Mr. Pierce.

"Martha," I said, "if there's anything . . ."

"Joe, I just can't tell you. It meant a great deal, just you being here. After the funeral . . ."

"What'll you do?"

"I really haven't thought." She gave a small, defenseless shrug of her thin shoulders. "We'll see. But, wherever I am, Joe, I'll never forget your kindness." She stood up quickly and kissed my cheek. "Good-bye for now."

"Good-bye, Martha. Take care. Good-bye, Mr. Pierce."

"Thanks for helping my girl, Joe. And good luck."

His girl. Certainly not mine. I walked out of the breakfast room and into the hall. Captain Richards stood talking to one of his troopers.

"Got a minute, Joe?"

"Sure. What's up?"

"We're just starting to get our act together. Come into my office." He led the way into a small paneled library I hadn't known about. Richards sat at the desk. I remained standing. "I didn't want to interrupt your talk with Pierce, Joe, but we have got problems."

This was not exactly blindingly new information.

"Anything I can do, Captain, I'll be glad to."

"I figured that."

Why did he figure that? What made him think I wasn't part of it, whatever it was? How did he know I wasn't about to cut and run? Maybe there was something about me that looked bone-foolish enough to like the idea of mysterious archers using my already beat-up body for midnight target practice. Or maybe he could read on my face the anger that had been building in me ever since Friday morning, slow, hot, steady anger that has to find its outlet or it'll just explode, and likely as not in the wrong place, at the wrong time, at the wrong person. Anyway, Richards looked efficient, with the low-key manner of a man who doesn't have to prove anything to anyone. Even a quick reading told me Richards would never let himself be drawn into the kind of running, losing game of psychological warfare that Al Coggin and Sheriff Billy played on the job and off it.

It gave me a good feeling to have Richards on the scene. And I needed all the good feelings I could get.

He leaned toward me. He's a compact man, maybe five-eight, but with one of those bullet-shaped bodies that would make you think twice about trying anything tricky on him.

"For starters," he began, running one hand over sandy hair

that was one stroke away from being a crew cut, "we haven't found the bullet. Or the gun either. Judging from the wound, it must have been a relatively small caliber, heavily rifled, perfectly shot. In and out, by way of his heart. We are dealing with a superb marksman. It had to be a one-shot situation, unless they had killers planted all through those woods, which seemed highly unlikely. We'll probably find the damn thing, but maybe not until spring. I've got two teams going over the area now—since yesterday—with metal detectors. So far we've come up with three cigarette lighters, eighty-three cents in change, and an empty box of Trojans."

"And what," I asked, "about my little pal from last night, Robin Hood, or William Tell, or whoever the hell he was?"

"His tracks are clear, but they don't tell us anything we couldn't have figured out for ourselves. He kept his skis on the whole time, and it's just about impossible to distinguish different kinds of ski tracks unless the bottoms are really screwed up, or they're older models, or cross-country skis. Whoever did it must have driven to the parking lot at the top of the condominiums in West Village. It'd be dark. He could unload his skis without anybody noticing, then climb diagonally up the hill and across the slope from there to here—a cinch in the dark. After the shot, we know what he did: hightailed it through Pierce's woods and across the slope in that direction. Thus, our brilliant deduction." The faintest flicker of a grin came and went from his lips. "He could have been at his car and on his way within five minutes."

"Leaving one skewered Bird."

"So to speak."

"Could our pals be staying right there in the West Village . . . or somewhere else nearby?"

"Of course they could. And, discreetly as possible, we're checking into that. Needless to say, there are some fancy folks residing in these parts who have to be handled with the proverbial kid gloves. And, in all reality, Joe, if anyone's lurking around the hotels like Silver Tree or El Dorado, with firearms and hunting bows, we'd be pretty likely to hear about it."

"It is just dawning on me that maybe I ought to keep a very low profile for a while." This was a lie. It had dawned on me in that chair lift, as I sat helpless while Blake Ross's lifeblood seeped out of him.

"I'm glad you said it first, Joe, because keeping you safe is right now my number-two problem, right after finding out who's behind all this."

"I don't want anything to endanger Joe's Place, Captain, or the people in it." *Including, let us not forget, its owner and proprietor.*

"You know you're getting a plainclothes trooper this afternoon?"

"I heard that. Thanks."

And I was grateful. But these funny little questions kept occurring to me, such as, would my own tame trooper be bulletproof? Arrowproof? How smart would he be? How honest? If the tried-and-true Far Right Conspiracy that has been the paranoid's plaything ever since they got the Kennedy boys had anything going for it, you'd have to start suspecting everyone from your dead grandmother to the Coors you had for lunch last Thursday. And I was just about prepared to do that.

"Well, Joe, our attitude about crime is very simple. We believe in preventive medicine. Nobody's less anxious to have you bothered than me. Believe that."

I do believe it, want to believe it, Captain dear, but it isn't you they're shooting at, is it? The anger rose a little higher in my gullet, which by then was something of an achievement.

"I do believe it. I also believe that arrow."

"Would you believe a little protective custody, a couple of weeks . . . somewhere else, until we wind all this up?"

"Negative. Thanks, but no thanks."

And would they have Rita with me? And what about the kids in Joe's Place, what about Rick and Charlie? It was too easy to imagine bombs, arson, machine guns in the night. And the thin, genuine-antique walls of Joe's Place. So charming. So vulnerable to a match.

"How about a little protective custody for the people who killed Blake Ross?"

"Cut it out, Joe. I can imagine the strain you're under. We're all under the same strain. But we are trying our damnedest."

Of course he was. How could I tell him his damnedest might not be enough?

"I'm sorry." I started with that and it didn't seem enough, so on it went, unnecessarily. "You get a little bugged after a day like yesterday. I know you're trying. And I will help. But I couldn't sit still in any kind of protective custody."

"You'll get one of my finest men, Joe."

"I look forward to his company. Can I have my car back now?"

"Sure. We're through. Want some company going back to town?"

Yes, please, three panzer divisions and the United States Air Force, in its entirety, for cover.

"No, thanks. I'll be all right. Knock wood."

"Okay, then. You'll get your watchdog after lunch. Meanwhile, sit tight. We'll be in touch."

"Thanks, Captain."

"You're sure you wouldn't like a few days in Denver?"

"In the slammer?"

"Under supervision. We do it all the time."

Not to me you don't.

"If these folks can get Blake Ross on a chair lift, what chance do I have anywhere? At least here I'm on my own terrain."

"You have to be the final judge of that, Joe."

I didn't like the way he said "final."

"I guess I do."

"Take care, Joe." Captain Richards, who was beyond doubt —if anything was beyond doubt anymore—an honorable man, gave me this valuable piece of advice as I rose to leave. And he smiled. It's always comforting when they smile. I walked out into the hallway and nearly bumped into Pierce coming from the opposite direction.

"Hi, Joe. Thought you'd gone."

"The captain had a couple of questions. Where's Martha?"

"Packing. Why don't you run up and say good-bye?" Good-bye to what? What pale worn-out useless dream was leaving town, that had never been invited to come? What very beautiful grief-stricken old childhood friend who might need some comforting, if anything ever could comfort someone like Martha after what had happened these last days?

"Thanks. I'll do that."

"You know the way?"

"Thanks to your hospitality of last night, yes, I do."

You didn't have to be psychic to detect a certain patronizing tone in the voice of Austin Pierce. It was the kind of tone that only comes with plenty of practice. I looked at the man and smiled and hoped the smile would hide the resentment Pierce had sown and reaped in me during the few hours he'd been in Aspen. Maybe the resentment came because I didn't like the influence he seemed to have on Martha. Maybe it was just because he's a type that gives me heartburn, the kind of man for whom mere money isn't ever enough, a man who needs strings to pull and favors to do and have done for him, and trims his machinations with false joviality, and decorates his lies with smiles. He smiled now, and held the smile a beat too long. I went upstairs, feeling his icicle eyes on me as I moved.

I knocked on the door of the big master bedroom where Blake Ross spent his last night on earth.

"Come in."

Martha was packing two big canvas suitcases, one obviously Blake's. She had changed into a dark-green wool suit for the journey to Washington. The hard morning light poured all around her from three big windows, bathing her in gold like some magic liquid.

Behind her, beyond the windows, the ski slopes of Snowmass were alive with skiers who moved in graceful swoops and arcs, brightly dressed and strangely silent, an enormous animated Christmas card that would never be delivered.

Martha hadn't done her hair yet.

It hung soft and loose on her shoulders. She had a lot of hair, beautiful hair, and I'd never seen it this way. Even as a kid Martha always had it compacted into some neat arrangement or other.

For a moment, a very long moment, I just stood there looking at her, blank as a bumpkin, trying to get a grip on myself. Because suddenly a great uninvited tide of sex came rising up in me, starting somewhere down below my toes and extending far, far over my muddled head. It surged through me hot and harsh until every part of me that could glow and tingle and throb and thirst for the touch of her was compounded into one crazy desire to cross that wide room and throw her back onto Austin Pierce's half-acre of bed and fuck her and fuck her and fuck her. I gulped. I'm not a gulper. Nor a rapist, either.

"What is it, Joe?" she asked, just in time. "You look a little funny."

"Just wondered if . . ."

"Joe. Dear. You've done too much already."

Nothing to what I would do, Martha, if I knew how, or what.

"You're sure you'll be okay?"

How could she be sure? How could she not be wondering whether they—the ever-present "they"—weren't gunning for her too? She straightened up from her packing and brushed the hair back from her cheek. It slid back like the opening-night curtain of a great drama, and I didn't even own a standee's ticket.

"Well . . ." Martha tried a small little smile, then thought better of it. "There's going to be some permanent damage, as the doctors like to say. I guess we both know that." She turned to the window then, and looked out at the skiers, then turned back to face me. "I have always believed in the future, Joe. To me the future is not someplace magical or mysterious. The future is a physical place, Joe, just like the past. Good things and bad things are buried there. If we look in the right places, and have luck, and try very hard, well, I do believe we can make the good things happen, pull them right out of that future, instead of the bad things. Once I thought I knew exactly how to do that. Now, as I stand here, I'm a lot less sure. But that doesn't mean I won't keep right on trying. That's the best any of us can do, don't you think?"

I thought.

She closed a suitcase with the quick finality of someone closing a book. Then Martha looked up at me, and this time the smile came for real.

"You go get some rest, Joe Bird. This is all going to get tougher before it gets better. But I will help, and Austin'll help, and, well, I will never be able to thank you, Joe. You'll be hearing from me."

"Take care, Martha."

"God bless."

I walked out of that bedroom and down the hall to the stairs. The hallway seemed a mile long.

6

You'd have to dig some to find a thing I hate more than making speeches. But that didn't stop me from gathering Rita and Charlie and Rick in a corner table at Joe's Place to tell them the score.

It was very important to keep my cool. Fat chance.

"Last night," I began in my usual subtle manner, "someone over at Pierce's place took a shot at me."

Rita jumped out of her chair as though it was electrified. "Joe!"

There were several messages in that small exclamation; surprise, of course, but also hurt that I hadn't told her, and fear, and maybe a tinge of something else, something I couldn't or didn't want to put my finger on right then. I knew then that I should have spelled it out on the phone last night, but I hadn't wanted to alarm her. So much for good intentions.

Rick frowned. Charlie said, "Wow!" which for Charlie is a major outburst of emotion.

Rita continued, "You never told us."

"I guess I didn't figure it would've stopped the arrow."

"Are you kidding? An arrow?" Rick had been leaning back in his chair, silent, slightly frowning, as if he were in the midst of solving some quaint metaphysical problem for himself and didn't much want to be disturbed. Rick was like that quite a lot. It was his way of hiding from the world. I had his full attention now. I continued.

"A nice big brass-tipped deer-hunting arrow, in fact. Ripped right through my Porsche's sheet metal. Charming to think what it might have done to my gut. But anyhow, it seems like someone quite determined has decided Aspen will be that much more scenic with me among the missing. The permanently missing. The thing is, I don't want to drag you kids into it."

I looked at each of them in turn, and kept my eyes on Rita.

"The next couple of days," I went on, "could get pretty lively around here. The state cops are giving me a live-in bodyguard, in fact he'll be showing up any minute now. But what I'd like would be if you kids would split for Vail—or Snowbird or anyplace—for a week or so. On the house. I'm going to be doing business as usual, against advice, and I really can handle it myself for a while. And, no kidding, I'll feel better about the whole thing if you're someplace . . . well, safer."

I didn't have to wait for their replies. They came faster than Robin Hood's arrow.

"Nope." This from Charlie.

"Not me." Rick.

"What kind of finks do you think we are, anyway?" That was from Rita.

Then they all began talking at once, even Charlie, and it dawned on me that this was a family council, whether I liked it or not. I liked it.

The details of that council were complicated and outrageous and touching and funny all at the same time. As family councils will be when they are evolving into councils of war. To sum it all up, they were not only not going to leave, they were personally going to track down the killers and render a variety of imaginative punishments that would have enthralled the torturers of the Inquisition.

Needless to say, I quickly put a lid on those particular plans. We couldn't look for anyone. We didn't know who to look for. My little feelings about Austin Pierce were based on the vaguest hint in Blake's last words, and on my own very private feelings about the man, and even combined, this added up to nothing. Furthermore, you'd have to be as rich and as well-connected as Pierce himself to keep him under any kind of surveillance. He used jets the way some people use Kleenex.

"We will," I said profoundly, "just have to sit tight."

"And," added Rick in an unfamiliar rasp which appeared to be his parody of the hired gun in every bad western movie, "keep our backs to the wall." He rose from his chair in a crouch, in perfect pantomime of the western quick-draw. "Pow! Pow!"

"Joe?" Rita's voice cut through the clowning, tense, low, urgent. "Why don't you take off from here?"

"They suggested that. The state police. It may be weird, but I feel safer here. On my own ground."

The phone rang, and Rick got it. It was for me. I picked up the receiver with the same enthusiasm with which I might have reached for a live rattlesnake.

The voice was familiar. "Mr. Bird?"

It was the short one.

"Would you say your grain elevators are getting rather full, Mr. Bird?"

"Right up to here. And so am I."

"In times of stress, Mr. Bird, it never helps to lose one's temper. After all. We are only trying to help."

"So do something helpful."

"Exactly."

"Exactly what?"

"Are you familiar with Glenwood Canyon?"

"Some."

"Dotsero?"

They were up to their old game again: monosyllables. Dotsero is a little town about halfway through the canyon on the way to Vail. The fact that games were being played didn't need explaining, even to me. But I had to wonder what the game really was, and who was playing it, even if the sure loser was named Joe Bird.

Gart continued, "Just after you pass the Dotsero turnoff, there is a small gas station on your left, with two house trailers parked next to it. At nine-forty-five exactly, tonight, we'll be waiting for you there."

Really. I'm going to be lured into the darkest, twistingist, loneliest canyon in Colorado by two very suspicious-looking finks who could just as well be telling me whatever they want to tell me over the phone right now.

"You'll have a long wait, then. I'm tired of playing games."

"Death is not a game, Mr. Bird."

"Avoiding my own death, Gart, is getting to look like the

only game in town. You really imagine I'm going to drive forty miles alone in that canyon when people are gunning for me right here in Aspen?"

"It's important, Mr. Bird. We need a conference."

"You can have one. Now. On the phone."

"Are you so naive, Mr. Bird, to imagine that your telephone is secure?"

Yes. You bet. I was that naive. And the thought of bugged phones, bugged bars and even bedrooms hit me hard and fast.

Gart paused for effect. Then he went on, "You must understand, Mr. Bird, that it is of the utmost importance that we keep our relationship secret. Not everyone in the, shall we say, official sector may be what he seems to be. Get it?"

I got it. "How do I know you're what you say?" *Come to think of it, they didn't really say.*

"We've been into that. Take my word for it, Mr. Bird, this is of the utmost importance. There is someone with us who wants very badly to meet you. His name is O'Leary."

"O'Leary!"

"Nine-forty-five, Mr. Bird." He ended his sentence with the mechanical click of a phone receiver being put to bed. *How in the devil did they know about O'Leary? If O'Leary was in fact with them. I had to hand them this: if they wanted to lure me into Glenwood Canyon, they sure picked the right lure.*

Glenwood Canyon, my ass.

Patrolman Lassiter showed up on the dot of noon like the clockwork man he was.

Lassiter was one of the new-breed cops, overstuffed with a college education and all the latest buzzwords about human behavior. I've got nothing against cops in general. I've got a lot against creeps, and Lassiter was a prime example of the species. Patrolman Lassiter had been left in the pickling jar a little too long. His face was pale, his hair lay sparse and lank on his tapering dome of a head, mean little eyes of no special color seemed to be winning a contest to meet each other in the center of his long, long-suffering face. The effect was not enhanced by his pink plastic eyeglasses, nor his thin, tight, pale-lipped mouth with its fascinating tendency to twitch involuntarily at unexpected moments. If I were picking a team, any team, Patrolman Lassiter would be the last possible choice.

That might have been the story of his life. Sure as hell, guarding Joe Bird couldn't be any supervising officer's idea of fun duty. I wondered who Lassiter had rubbed the wrong way in order to draw duty at Joe's Place. In a foxhole, I'd take Al Coggin anytime.

Lassiter spoke. "How do you do, Mr. Bird?"

Funny you should ask.

His handshake was thin and tense as the rest of him, more claw than hand. But, what the hell, he was my bodyguard, I would have to live in his pocket for a few days, why not try to make the best of it? I managed a smile. I managed to speak. "I'm fine, thanks, give or take an assassination attempt or two. It's good to have you here."

I introduced him around, showed him where he'd be bunking—with Charlie and Rick. Then I got us both a cup of coffee and took him upstairs for a talk.

The first words out of Lassiter's mouth gave him a big head start on the wrong track. "You realize, of course," he began, sitting up as straight and prim as anyone can sit on my big soft leather couch, "that it will be impossible for you to keep the bar open until all this has been cleared up?"

My first instinct was to get tough with him. Then I decided it was more a question of educating this creepy little bureaucrat than startling him with naughty language.

"I've already discussed that with Captain Richards. We both agree that more can be accomplished by keeping up a normal front."

"But you're a target."

"Thanks. I do realize that. Tell me where I won't be. Do you have the answer to that one? Because, if you do, you win the Sherlock Holmes Award of this and every month."

"I'm only thinking of your safety, Mr. Bird."

"So am I. And Joe's Place is going to stay open even if I have to pour beer for every murderer west of the Mississippi, pal, don't have any doubts about that. Hell, man, it's my living."

I could see his already curdled face curdling even more. The upper left lip suddenly took on a life of its own and twitched three times in rapid succession. I couldn't take my eyes off it.

"Joe's Bar is your living, with which you pay your taxes, which pays my salary, right? Well, if that's going to be your attitude, Mr. Bird—"

"Joe, please. And the name of the establishment is Joe's Place."

"Joe. Then it isn't going to be easy to help you."

"No. I don't suppose it will be."

I looked at the man and tried to think of ways to help him. Lassiter had the sad look of someone for whom a lot of things in life hadn't turned out right. Or maybe some people are just born that way. I hope not. In the end, I said very little, and led him downstairs to unpack.

Lassiter's first glimpse of Charlie and Rick was what my Aunt Polly used to call a caution. I guess maybe their hair wasn't short enough for him, or maybe their manner was a little too easygoing, or simply that they were both good-looking guys who drew girls into Joe's Place like honeybees to the hive. Maybe Lassiter guessed that not everything Rick and Charlie smoked came from Winston-Salem, North Carolina. Whatever the reason, it seemed, that first afternoon of Lassiter's regime at Joe's Place, that he spent more time watching my bartenders than me.

We opened for business right on schedule, at three-thirty.

One thing you can say about violent death: it does great things for your bar business. By five the customers were three deep at the bar, and the noise level was somewhere around New Year's Eve, which is saying a lot.

And there were reporters.

I'd already agreed with Richards not to say a word to any of them. My "No comment" was a pure and beautiful thing. But the reporters came anyway, seemed to like the place, seemed to use it as a kind of headquarters. I suppose there was always the chance I'd spill something, that another attempt might be made on me, on the premises, who knows? They weren't bad guys.

Saturday at Joe's Place is a pretty cheerful thing anytime of the year. This Saturday the festivities had a special edge on them. There was a tension riding on the hilarity, a crackle in the air that was more than the promise of snow. And somehow I managed to be in the thick of it, faking confidence, making jokes, slapping backs, kissing ladies, the jolly innkeeper right out of Chaucer. Ho, ho, ho.

The afternoon worked its merry way into evening, and I hung in there for every fun-filled minute of it. Two cheeseburgers and a glass of red wine were my supper. I felt like I hadn't eaten in days, and the fact was, I hadn't. So I sipped my wine and feigned good cheer and watched the not very cleverly disguised Patrolman Lassiter in his seedy civvies grimly performing the letter, if not the spirit, of his duty, sipping ginger ale at the bar.

And, of course, I thought of the two other creeps who had so lately and so uninvitedly landed in my life. And how they'd be waiting in the canyon.

From time to time Lassiter would put down his lukewarm ginger ale and walk out of Joe's Place, presumably checking the area for communist tanks, hordes of Visigoths, and other lurking menaces. For one wicked moment I wanted to be a lurking menace on any street patrolled by Patrolman Lassiter.

He left for the third of these patrols about eight-thirty.

When Lassiter came back in, ten minutes later, I eased my way up to him at the bar. "Is everything okay?" I asked in my best gangster-movie imitation tough-guy-ese.

"As well as can be expected."

Those were precisely the words the doctors had used when my mother was dying of cancer.

It was at exactly that moment when Joe Bird decided he needed a quick, refreshing drive in the country.

It was eight-forty on the nose when I slipped out the back door to my parking lot. Ask me why I did it and you won't get a nice, logical answer. Certainly not because I'd been asked to. I hope not because of the intimidation built into Gart's clipped voice. The fact that they'd promised me O'Leary had a lot to do with it. Probably it was O'Leary plus a combination of my massive, unreasoning distaste for Lassiter added to the fact that I'd been caged inside all afternoon. Or maybe it was Martha, my only half-submerged desire to make something happen, to get the termites out of the woodwork, to purge the atmosphere once and for all.

I'll never learn.

It was a fine, reckless feeling to elude my keeper with his mealy mouth and slightly mad rabbit's eyes.

The Porsche's engine purred and rumbled happily as I eased her out onto Highway 82 and west toward Glenwood Springs.

There's an easier way to Vail and Denver than through the canyon. You can drive over Independence Pass through Leadville, and the way is more direct. But the pass is closed all winter. The canyon way leads you on two long legs of a triangle, first west to Glenwood Springs, then back east again through the canyon itself toward Vail and, after that, Denver.

It's worth the extra miles. Glenwood Canyon is one of God's happier inventions in the field of sculpture, a deep, narrow, very dramatic rock trough cut sharp by that same swift Colorado River that ultimately produced Grand Canyon a few hundred miles down the road.

I've always liked the little canyon better. It's more intimate.

Glenwood Canyon has the same intricate rock spires, the same French-pastry many-colored layer upon layer of sedimentary rock, and the same practically opalescent ever-changing purple shadows on the red and gray and brown and yellow stone. You get the same sense of racing eternity in Glenwood Canyon, and losing.

The canyon was here before us and it will go on after we're gone, and the wild Colorado wind howling down the thousand layers of stone and dancing with the white spray in the rapids will hardly know the difference.

Glenwood Canyon is dark and narrow even in daylight, and for the most part the river runs through it fast and deep. On one side the Union Pacific cut a shelf for their main line through to Salt Lake City. On the other side, a matching low-cut shelf holds the two narrow lanes of Highway 70, a tricky sidewinder of a road that leaves you no alternatives: on your left, driving toward Vail, is a wall of rock. On your right is a sheer drop into the river.

Nobody had to tell me what a perfect trap it made.

I drove slower than usual, maybe ten miles over the limit. And I kept thinking of all the things I didn't know about the people who were so earnestly trying to kill me. For instance, I had no idea just what O'Leary's theory was. Nor any way but this to find out. They way Blake used his name made him sound like someone Blake knew well, trusted, consulted. Yet Martha knew him only vaguely. Well, maybe tonight I'd find out. Maybe.

The night seemed to get darker as I drove farther and farther from Aspen.

At night, in winter, Glenwood Canyon is about as dark as the far side of the moon, and almost as empty. You'll see a big truck now and then, an occasional rancher in a pickup, sometimes a late party of skiers coming back from Vail. But many's the time I've driven the entire thirty-some-mile length of the canyon, coming back from a long day's skiing at Vail, and hardly seen another car. So much the faster.

It was a peaceful night, which until lately was about the only kind of night his part of Colorado was used to. The wheel felt good in my hands; the smooth precise murmurings of the Porsche filled the silence with expensive reassurance.

It was a few minutes after nine when I turned off the bridge at Glenwood Springs and drove into the canyon.

The big gray Lincoln must have picked me up about then, but wandering thoughts or just plain stupidity kept me from paying much attention to his headlights until we were quite a ways out of town and it became obvious that he was tailing me.

Or maybe he bided his time until he was sure we were well-isolated.

Once he caught my eye, we began a little mating dance of spinning rubber and rocketing steel. When I slowed, he slowed. If I sped up, so did he. Once I came up on a truck and did some fancy passing. And so did he.

The traffic thinned out as we got into the canyon, and pretty soon it was only him and me. Exactly the way he wanted it.

I kept an eye on my rearview mirror as often as the tricky road would let me. With no headlights behind the Lincoln to silhouette the driver, it was hard to make him out: one man, big, too big to be Gart, maybe the other one. I really couldn't tell.

The Lincoln was big and fast, but my car was faster and nimbler. In any race, I'd win. But it wasn't a race yet. I forced myself not to panic. After all, I didn't exactly have it in writing that the guy really was tailing me. It only seemed that way. And even if he was tailing me deliberately, maybe he was on our side.

Then he tried to run me into the river.

When you get right down to it, it's hard to believe that someone wants you dead, now, quickly, by any means available.

Up until that moment the whole adventure had had a kind of dreamlike quality, nightmarelike, more accurately, but lacking the reality that only comes when here is this man, in plain sight, actually trying to make you dead.

Well, the dreamlike quality evaporated in about three cold-sweat seconds. O'Leary, hell. All these guys had waiting for me was the cold, dark riverbed.

The Lincoln's headlights came up from nowhere and filled my car, high beams glaring. I could hear his engine racing. He was cutting in on me from the opposite lane, all set to bop me like a penalty croquet ball into the dark, swift river fifty feet below.

If he had been smart enough to kill his lights, if the Porsche had less than a jackrabbit's reflexes, if Joe Bird were half a second slower on the downshift and acceleration, there might be no end to this story.

I floored it. The Porsche did its duty, and adrenaline did the rest.

My car shot into the night as the Lincoln swerved from its attack position to take up the chase. He had lost his one advantage of surprise. His tires wailed as he yanked the big sedan back from the shoulder of the hardtop and stepped on the gas.

The only thing in my alleged head was to outrun him all the way to Denver, if that was what it took. Then a sign flashed by: DANGER. FALLING-ROCK ZONE. And a nasty little idea grew in my brain like a black flower.

The canyon loops and wiggles like snakes making love, if snakes make love.

Thank God there weren't any straightaways, because the Lincoln might well have caught me then. But on curves it wasn't even a contest. The Porsche drifted around those curves flat and sure and easy at better than seventy miles an hour. I'd downshift for better control and faster pullout from the turns, the timing instinctive, the car responding to my urgency with the special grace of all finely made machines, quick as thought, more than the sum of its parts.

The distance between me and the deadly gray Lincoln got wider and then wider yet. Suddenly the canyon road took a great sweep outward and I could see the Lincoln lurching around another curve, two curves back.

Now was the time, and maybe the only time, to put my plan to the test.

I cut off my headlights, and smiled, because that same bright moon that had helped the bow-and-arrow man the night before was going to help Joe Bird now.

Praying for silence, I shifted down through two more gears, to brake the car, then just touched the brakes and threw the Porsche into a power drift of 180 degrees just on the far side of that big, looping curve. It was a risk, but risks with Porsches are not like other risks. The car swung tight and true and ended up ticking in darkness on the shoulder of the opposite lane, facing back toward Aspen.

I left the motor running and jumped out.

The guys who put up the falling-rock sign were honest men: the roadside was lousy with them. I chose two rocks a little bigger than bricks and ran to the farthest extreme of the curve just as the Lincoln's headlights began glaring off the steep rock outcropping on the other side of the canyon.

I was counting on the driver's being on the far edge of control.

I counted right.

He came screeching and careening around that curve, wrestling the wheel in a kind of mad desperation that had nothing to do with good driving or control. Wonderful. I practically walked into him before he saw me, and by the time he saw me, rock number one was sailing through the air in a lovely parabola that ended by smashing right through the driver's side of the big, expensively tinted windshield of the Lincoln.

It was Vega.

He had the bad taste to scream.

The big gray car staggered like a wounded creature, shuddering as Vega's hands froze on the wheel. He must have slammed on the brakes, because the Lincoln went into a wild, acrobatic skid, first lurching sideways in my direction, narrowly missing my Porsche, half-climbing the wall of rock beyond the shoulder of the opposite lane, bouncing off with a great agonized screeching of metal stressed beyond endurance.

By now the windshield was mostly a big black hole, and I couldn't see Vega at all. He might have had a chance to jump.

The Lincoln careened off the canyon wall and ricocheted across the empty two-lane road to the river's edge, where there was nothing at all to hold it back except maybe Vega's last wishes.

It happened very fast, but in my mind it runs on slow motion: the great gray car seeming to float across that highway and over the brink, arcing through the clean moonlit Colorado night, and landing with a huge splash in the iced black depths of the raging Colorado River fifty feet below.

I stood dumb at the edge of the road. The splash wet my face and mixed with tears I hadn't known were there.

The tears were not for the man I'd killed, but they were filled with sorrow nevertheless, sorrow and possibly rage at this uninvited fate that had suddenly made me kill.

I stood there in a kind of shock, one fist clenched, the other still holding the second, unthrown rock. The canyon glittered with moonlight, and as I fought with the horror of what I had done, only the rushing, splashing river served to remind me of things alive, of going places, doing things. I saw it all again, standing silent on the river's edge: the gray Lincoln shot across that empty road once more and seemed to hang in the moonlight for a moment, already the ghost of a car, transfixed, its twin headlight beams dancing with a kind of unexpected, mocking gaiety on the opposite canyon wall. Then the great car nosed down and hit the water with a sound more like thunder then splashing, a hollow, thick noise, vast and primitive and final in the empty night. The big car wallowed in the river for a moment, then sank in a rush of bubbles. The brilliant, high-beamed headlights lived on after the car and its driver had died. I could see them sinking slowly, down and down, an eerie double glow five and then ten and then twenty feet under. As the car sank deeper, all I could see of it was those beams. They wavered as the current tugged at the bulk of the car, pulling until those unfaltering beams edged out toward the mainstream, pointing uselessly in the general direction of Mexico.

I couldn't tell you how long I stood there. It was a second piece of luck that no one came along. The cold night wind that had long since dried my face now woke me from this trance. I noticed the rock in my left hand with a shudder and dropped it where I stood.

Then I walked slowly across the road and climbed into my car. I sat there, shaking a little, my hands tight on the steering wheel, thinking. Trying to think, anyway. After a time I flicked the Porsche into gear and headed back to Aspen.

My first impulse was not to tell anybody. Wrong, like so many of my first impulses. Of course I'd have to tell all about it, and in detail, and with names and times and places. The time had come to call up the hounds after Mr. Gart and his former sidekick, Vega. I wound the Porsche back through Glenwood Canyon at an easy fifty-five. Driving on eggs. I met no one, in either direction, until the usual traffic of Glenwood Springs cluttered the road.

Across the river, the brightening moon sparkled off the tracks of the Union Pacific and lit up the foaming rapids in between. Overhead, immense soaring, convoluted spires of rock loomed darkly like the ruin of some forgotten ancient palace of a race of giants. The night was heavy with the empty grandeur of it.

And all I could think about was, do rocks hold fingerprints in moving water?

7

You could hear Joe's Place a block away by the time I wandered in through the back door around eleven. The happy-crowd noises seemed even louder by contrast to the cryptic silence in the canyon.

Rita edged up to me through the crowd. The look on her face told me something about the look on my face, so I tried to change it into a nice big smile. Failure.

"Where were you?" she asked in a low voice that was edged with concern. "Lassiter's getting more hysterical by the minute."

I would be jovial. "The young fogy? Has to be that guy's mission in life, being hysterical. Everyone needs a hobby. I went for a drive. Stir-crazy. Acute Lassiteritis."

She wasn't buying it. "Are you all right, Joe?"

"As well as can be expected." I hated to do that, but this wasn't the time or the place to go into details.

"You're taking chances."

"Hell, everything's a chance." This little homily, specially invented for the occasion, was proving itself all too true, all too quickly. Rita looked me up and down with an unreadable stare, then decided not to take it any further. I was glad about that.

"Yeah," she said quietly, "maybe it is." Then she turned and lost herself in the mob.

I went over to the bar and helped myself to a big glass of the house red. Lassiter was standing in a corner of the back room, alone. He didn't even have his glass of ginger ale. He soon caught me in one of the jerky little sweeps his eyes made every few seconds, scanning the room from side to side like a radar antenna gone mad. He stalked over and signaled me into the bunkroom behind the kitchen.

I sprawled back on Charlie's bed and saluted him with my wineglass. "To the triumph of justice." The wine was soft and warming on my tongue. I smiled as it wended its happy way into my trembling gut.

Lassiter, needless to say, was not amused. "That was a pretty irresponsible thing to do, Mr. Bird."

I'd been demoted. Just this afternoon I had him calling me Joe.

"You were gone," he continued, schoolmaster to small, naughty child, "nearly two hours. Anything might have happened. I simply cannot be accountable for your welfare if anything like this happens again."

Accountable. That was truly the name of the game with these boys. Not, was it right or wrong, or good or bad, but did the bottom line add up nice and neatly?

Lassiter stood there, thin and rigid, all strings quivering, a textbook hysteric. All of a sudden, out of the blue, I began to feel sorry for my bodyguard. I had this quick sad vision of his entire life to date, and it was filled with mothers and aunts who hadn't baked cookies for him, and teams he hadn't made, and girls who hadn't sacked out with him, and promotions he might never get. All wrapped up in this skinny pillar of repression and nameless tensions standing taut and flustered before me.

"Lassiter," I asked in my cheeriest voice, "tell me something. What's your name?"

"John."

He said the name tentatively, as if there might be something wrong with it.

"John, then. John." I savored it. "Perfectly good name. Call me Joe, would you? All this formality gives me the creeps. Okay?"

"All right. Joe."

I might have been drawing my name out of him with pliers.

"Fine. Now, John, I have a little story to tell you. But first we both need a drink."

At least one of us did. My wineglass had gone empty on me, as if by magic.

"Oh," said Lassiter, twitching violently. "No. That is, I couldn't."

"Ha. Can't handle it, eh?"

"I can handle it," he said rather primly, "but it's just . . . just that . . ."

"You're on duty, right? Duty, comma, dereliction of. I know it well, John, and don't worry your little head about such a thing. Fact is, part of your duty is to mix with the locals. And what the locals are mixing, old buddy, ain't branch water."

The devil made me do it.

"Well . . ."

"Consider it in the line of duty, John." I led him to the bar and laid on a big pitcher of Dominics. Dominics are the very special invention of a man I knew named Dominic. And what they won't do for after dinner, the Bomb didn't do for Hiroshima. A Dominic is an irresistible mixture of half Benedictine and half Galliano, and the result, stirred with crushed ice, is guaranteed to stoke all the appropriate fires in man, woman, or beast. I put the pitcher and two iced martini glasses on a tray and led John Lassiter through the jovial crowd and up to my living room.

There I lit the fire and filled two glasses and handed one to him. "Down the hatch, John."

"To your health."

The irony of this escaped him. But anyway, he drank. John Lassiter sipped the pale golden Dominic with birdlike caution, the court taster of an unpopular king.

"It's very smooth," he said.

Righty-ho, John. Smoothness is all.

"I just killed a man."

"You *what*?" He choked on his drink and sputtered.

"At least, I think I did."

"You're kidding me. This is some kind of joke."

"He went into the Colorado River at about sixty miles an hour in a big Lincoln sedan that sank like a rock. So he is very likely to be dead. Or at least seriously unwell. By now."

"You're not kidding." John Lassiter took another sip of his drink, and then another.

"John, you are the representative of justice in my humble abode. I wouldn't kid you. Not about this. I give myself up. It was self-defense. Truly."

I refilled his glass and mine, and told him the full story of

Gart and Vega and the phone call, the chase through the canyon and the crash. I told it as quickly and as unemotionally as I could, thinking all the while that I'd no doubt have to repeat the performance any number of times to any number of fuzz-type officials. A little practice never hurt.

Lassiter sat back on the big leather sofa, sipping his drink with increasing appetite. When I finished, he looked at me in silence for a minute, his pale eyes expressionless behind their pale pink plastic glasses.

"Wow," he said.

"Exactly," I replied. "Of course, it was self-defense."

"Of course. No question. But I was thinking, Joe: it was pretty brave, too."

"And pretty stupid: remember, I more or less believed those guys and their silly code." And that Bob O'Leary was with them.

"They could be for real, you know. Funnier things happen."

"Not to Joe Bird, they don't. You mean, those guys could really be feds of some kind and still try to kill me?"

"Don't quote me, Joe. But this is a very weird situation. Very, very weird."

He drained his glass. Dominic's concoction was working its magic spell. Maybe a little too well.

I refilled his glass and part of mine. "The most involvement I've ever had with the law is speeding tickets."

"The question," said Lassiter, "is what to do next."

"How about retrieving that car, and whoever may be in it?"

He seemed relieved that the suggestion came from me. I had a feeling that maybe John Lassiter had spent too much time being accountable, and not enough time making suggestions.

"Is there a phone up here?"

He acted efficiently then, calling for Richards, who was out, and filing a basic witness-to-accident report that would get the action level of the state police going on locating the Lincoln and checking its ownership and the identity of the man behind the wheel. Assuming he'd still be identifiable by the time they got to him.

I took another swallow of the Dominic, and it poured its

icy warmth down my throat like all the healing potions in the history of medical science. A soft warm explosion hit my stomach and spread inch by inch down my legs and up my arms and all through me with the glorious ease of a skier—me, naturally, floating through new powder. I sipped again, and refilled my glass and his.

Lassiter finished his call and came back to the fire. "Everything's set. They'll start dragging the river at daybreak. So far as they know, you saw an accident. Stopped your car, but couldn't stop the crash. That'll account for any telltale tire marks that could be traced to your Porsche. And as soon as I can get to Richards, we'll look into the Gart and Vega thing. Very quietly, of course."

"Of course. I lifted my glass in silent appreciation of Lassiter's efforts. But where my mind was, was somewhere black and cold at the bottom of the Colorado River, and I could feel the raw scraping in my bones as the frigid current tugged and shoved a big expensive hunk of gray-enameled metal downstream toward Mexico with a fresh-trapped cargo of death.

Lassiter's voice cut in on my grim reverie. "You will have to make a statement, naturally, Joe. We'll take care of that tomorrow."

"What will I say?" How much will I admit? They could throw the book at me. They probably could lock me up then and there."

"They'd probably like to, for your own safety." He actually giggled.

"I suppose if I say that'd happen over my dead body, you'd take it as satire?"

"It may be hard for you to believe this, Joe, but I do understand."

"Thanks." *Thanks for what?*

"You're welcome. Before you make any statement, talk to Richards."

"I hope to." *If I live that long.*

"First, they have to find the body. And they might not."

"Fat chance."

Something sparkled and shifted in the pale eyes of John Lassiter. It could have been the drinks. It could have been anything. "You never know."

What was he trying to tell me? That the body might be found and disposed of? That they really might not find it? One more time I replayed the crash in its usual, dreadful slow motion. The big hole in the windshield. I could imagine the car filling with water, the current seeping in somehow, forcing the body out that hole. A body could be carried miles, maybe hundreds of miles, by that rushing current. Into Arizona, into the Grand Canyon. Even into Mexico. Swell. I wasn't just a murderer, I was an interstate, maybe international murderer.

Something was changing in Lassiter.

Suddenly he unwound his long tense body until all the many hard edges seemed to melt away and he curled back against the soft leather couch like so much limp spaghetti. His glass was empty. I refilled it, got up, and left him with what remained in the pitcher. He spoke.

"Attractive room."

"Thanks."

"Most attractively decorated."

"It's comfortable."

" 'S most attractive."

"All right, John, old pal, just you hang in here and relax. I've got a few people to talk to. I'll just be downstairs, right?"

" 'S right." He nodded happily and smiled into the cool golden depths of his glass.

I went back downstairs to Joe's Place and took up where I'd left off, laughing, joking, mingling with the crowd. The Dominics helped. I tried to pretend it was just another Saturday night at Joe's Place. I would have given quite a lot for that pretense to be true.

There came a moment when I saw my face in the big old gilt-framed mirror behind the bar. It's the only face I have; I don't pay much attention to it. But that Saturday night I looked at my face in the mirror and saw the face of a killer looking back.

They say that once you have intentionally killed someone you are changed finally and forever. I looked into the mirror and saw the same old face, no dripping fangs, no shifty eyes, no horns. But still I stared at the mirror. Waiting.

Then I asked for a glass of plain ice water.

Along about midnight Al Coggin and Billy Medina wandered in, off duty at last, tired and wanting a beer.

"Any news?"

Billy greeted my question with the God-preserve-me-from-the-inevitable expression of some early Christian martyr. I gathered from this subtle display that he had heard the question a few times before that day.

"If we'd been having adventures like yours, Joe, we might know a lot more."

Did they know about tonight? And if so, who told them? And what should I do about it? I simply felt too tired to go into it if it didn't need going into. So I brought them their beers and asked about the bullet.

"Not a trace," said Billy, sipping his Coors with the first real expression of pleasure I'd seen on his face since the killing. "You know," he went on, "how deep the base is up there. Maybe thirty-five, forty feet. Solid snow. And every time the goddamn metal detector goes off, we've got to dig. The ski patrol's furious. The trail looks like a minefield. But the fact is, Joe, once the thing went through the man, it couldn't of traveled far. I mean, that bullet was spent."

It sure was.

Al Coggin swirled his beer, drank a little and looked at me. "Richards tell you his theory about a target pistol?"

His tone was all I needed to tell me how little Al thought of the theory.

"No."

"What," asked Sheriff Billy, reasserting his lost dominance of the talk, "is the distance between chairs?"

"About twenty-five feet," answered Al, all duty and submission. "But the angle's wrong. And the people in the chair immediately behind Joe and the senator were this lady from California and her eight-year-old kid."

"And the people behind her would have seen."

"And anyway, we're pretty sure we've found the hiding place."

If Al wasn't capping Billy's thoughts, Billy was sure to cap Al's.

"Clump of firs," Al began, looking at me, "down right where you suggested. Lots of cover—"

"But a clear shot at the lift." Billy jumped in, his enthusiasm somehow renewed.

"Tracks?" My question.

"Too many. That's the trouble." Billy resumed his usual control over proceedings. "They're all over the damn place. Tourists."

I sat there being polite, and wished they'd go away. It had been a long day and a longer night, and all I wanted right then was for it to end. Happily, if possible, but anyway to end. The magic spell of the Dominics was wearing thin. I contemplated coffee, then uncontemplated it. The beers being slowly, slowly sipped by Billy and Al began to look very good to me. I excused myself for a minute and got one.

Al was the first to speak up when I got back. "What I can't figure out," he said, as if he had everything else in the case down pat, "is, why the bow and arrow?"

"That," said Billy, in the full wisdom of his high office, "is the question."

"It seems," I remarked, "like Aspen is just filled with questions like that these days. And not a tremendous number of answers."

They both looked at me as though I'd slapped them. If I could have swallowed my unthinking words, I would have, and gladly. I like Billy and Al, and the last thing in my mind was to insult them.

"We're doing our best, Joe." This came from Al, who stood up, a sure sign I'd truly put my foot in it.

"Look. I know that. And I'm sorry if I sound jumpy. Fact is, I am jumpy. Being a target and all." I could have said it better. If I were someone else, and this was another day, and I hadn't just killed a man.

"Sure," said Billy Medina, for once in his life taking a cue from Al and rising, leaving the beer half-drunk. "Listen, Joe, we'd better get going. Long day tomorrow." Good show. One cop drunk and the other two mad at me. The killers couldn't have planned it better themselves.

The crowd was thinning out a little, like it always does after twelve. Serious skiers get up early, and most of my crowd are skiers. Out of the corner of my eye I got a glimpse of Charlie helping Lassiter down the stairs and into the bunkroom. I looked at my watch. Twelve-twenty-nine.

So it was Sunday. The third day since Blake and Martha Ross strolled into Joe's Place and changed my life forever.

I finished my beer and had another. We closed a little after two, with no unusual happenings. I helped the kids clean up, and locked everything that could be locked, and was pouring myself a final beer when Charlie and Rick came clattering out of the kitchen with their arms filled with pots and pans and empty bottles.

"What," I asked, dumbfounded, "in hell is this?"

Charlie grinned his mile-wide grin. "Distant Early Warning System reporting for duty, sir. Let the bastards try and get in a window or up the stairs without we hear 'em, right?"

It made sense.

"Right." I laughed, we all did, but inside I wasn't laughing. Thank God the kids were thinking, because I obviously wasn't. I sent Rita upstairs and helped them finish their booby-trapping. In a childish way, it was fun. Before we were through, all the downstairs doors and windows of Joe's Place were thoroughly lined with large noise-making obstacles. Chairs tilted against the doorknobs, and large pots on the chairs, and bottles in the pots. The staircase looked like a tinker's going-out-of-business sale. With all lights out, anyone with dark designs on Joe Bird was going to have to come down the chimney—which was hot—to get me unawares.

I backed up the stairs, taking care not to spill the beer. The way those stairs looked, and tired as I felt, that beer would have to do me till tomorrow.

Rita was sitting on the big brown leather sofa by the fireplace, just where I left Lassiter, who was now spending a lot of time in the downstairs men's room. Too many Dominics.

She looked very soft and Victorian in her old-fashioned bathrobe of blue cotton flannel printed all over with sprigs of white flowers, her long blond hair falling soft below her shoulders, long slim legs drawn up childishly underneath her for warmth. She leaned back and stared dreamily into the big glass of red wine. This was exceptional for Rita. She hardly drinks at all.

"It's been," she began softly, "quite a day. You look like hell."

"Thanks." I managed a smile. She didn't know it yet, but this was a killer's smile. "I always speak well of you. And, after all, my dear, how often do you get to meet someone as charming as old Lassiter?"

That was the note: keep it cool, keep it playful, don't let the wounds show.

"Isn't he something? Reminds me of *I Was a Teenage Zombie*." He just thrills me to pieces, Joe."

"I think he's kind of cute myself."

"What happened tonight?"

Trust old Rita. Pulling nary a punch.

"Why?"

"You looked funny when you came back."

There went what little was left of my cool. I sat next to her on the soft couch. I took her hand. I felt like dirt. "What would you say," I asked, meaning it, "if I told you I killed a man?"

So I told her. I took her through it slowly, in detail, in more detail than I'd bothered to give Lassiter. And while I spoke, I could feel the simple fact of telling my guilt making me feel better. As it made her feel worse. It was like passing on an infection, and all the time the words came out, I knew it was wrong, selfish, immoral to be laying on this nice simple girl a big mixed-up burden of hate and death that she hadn't asked for and sure as hell didn't need. But none of these fine secret sentiments kept me from finishing the tale. Such as it was.

By the time I'd finished, she was crying. I could have predicted that, even though Rita cries as seldom as she drinks. Tonight it was all coming out.

"Hey. What's all this?"

"Joe, I'm scared."

"Me too."

"What are we going to do?"

That "we" had a way of creeping into Rita's conversation lately, in a manner well-calculated to raise the alarm in the heart and mind of any self-respecting play-the-field bachelor. Somehow, that night it made sense.

"There's not a whole lot we can do. The cops really are trying. I guess we just kind of sit tight for a while."

"Can I help?"

"You help," I said, bending to kiss her, "just by being here." I set the beer down and took a very hot shower. It didn't wash death away. Rita was sitting just as I'd left her. There was hardly a dent in her wine. I sat down next to her, liking the feel of the warm leather on my bare skin, put one arm around her, and began playing with all that hair. Death and sex are more closely related than most of us ever have a chance to find out. I had a taste of the beer, and that felt good too.

Rita must have felt my hand on her neck, but when she spoke, it was as though she was talking to some small amphibian who lived at the bottom of her wineglass. "Tell me," she said in a voice whose quiet detachment had very little to do with Rita's easygoing everyday way of speaking, "about her."

"Her who?"

But I knew who. And I didn't want to darken the night further with useless dreams or excuses or apologies for Martha. I looked at the back of Rita's head and thought: *You don't have the right. Keep off the grass. Don't pick the flowers.* Maybe she did have the right, whatever that was. That and twelve bucks would get her a day's lift ticket to Ajax Mountain.

"That," I said, sipping the beer, "is a long story. Martha's a very special lady."

"Childhood sweethearts?"

"They met the first year after she got out of college."

"I meant you, dummy."

"No." I said it too quickly. "Not really."

Then she did look at me. Rita turned on the sofa, and her eyes met mine. She took the smallest possible sip of wine. "You wouldn't say that," she said, even softer now, "if you'd seen yourself looking at her that night."

"I was kind of shocked. It'd been years." *Shall I tell you how many, Rita? To the day and the hour?*

"Until that night, I never would have believed you could need anyone."

I tried on a small laugh. It didn't fit. "I'm that hard-hearted?"

She reached out with one hand and touched my cheek, a soft touch, a touch that burned. "You're so good at being alone."

"I've had a lot of practice." Almost fifteen years. Fifteen

years of building walls and burning bridges. Fifteen years of hiding behind mountains when a haystack would probably have done the job. Of learning to love a loner's sport and then blowing even that because of one chance taken, the famous one too many. And then learning not to take chances, learning to be cool, to glide down the well-marked trails looking good for the tourists, taking it easy and taking the easy laughs and the easier girls and the money that came easier than it should have, considering my relatively simple needs. And pretending all the while that inside me beat a bulletproof heart wrapped in a drip-dry soul.

There was no way to explain this to Rita, even if she had the right. I didn't try.

"You're mad."

"Hell no. Tired."

"I asked the wrong question." She stated the fact of it. I stood up. So did she. I kissed her softly.

"Tonight," I said through the kiss, "there is no such thing as the right question." I flicked off the last light and we melted into the big old brass bed.

8

The crash on the stairs and the shouts and the gunshot all came at once, maybe an hour later.

I hit the floor running, buck-naked, not even stopping to think if there was a weapon handy. I've never kept a gun in Joe's Place: they scare me more than they'd scare most burglars. The crash and the racket had come from downstairs. I had sense enough not to rush down into what might have been a gunfight, but instead flattened myself against the wall and slowly reached for the stairwell light switch.

Someone moaned.

The first light showed us the action was all over. John Lassiter lay sprawled about halfway up the stairs with his left leg twisted under him at a crazy angle. Broken. Rick stood over him holding a pistol, Lassiter's own pistol it turned out, that he'd been carrying when he started creeping up my stairs. That he'd shot as he fell.

Lassiter moaned again. His eyes were closed.

Rita appeared behind me, armed with the fire tongs. She looked over my shoulder at the not-very-funny comedy below. "Terrific."

It made me smile. Rita can usually do that. Then I stopped smiling. This was obviously going to be the longest night in the world. I should have been wiped out. Somehow I was getting a second wind.

"What happened?" I asked of no one in particular, realizing as the words formed how unlikely it was that they'd ever be answered.

"What happened?" The echo came from Charlie, last on the scene, ambling into the bar looking like a road-company Shakespearean comic in long red ski underwear.

"Our hero kind of blew his cool, it looks like." Rick said

this thoughtfully, not quite believing the words, his own practiced cool very much intact. The gun, held almost casually, was pointing not at all casually right at Lassiter's contorted face. "Now, what," said Rick in the same quiet tone, "do you suppose he was after?"

Good question.

I suggested that Rita go back to bed, and went back myself, but only to dress. Then I called the state police and told them to come pick up the pieces.

Rick and Charlie and I sat around the corner table sipping beers, waiting. We'd taken it on ourselves to unwind old Lassiter from his painful resting place on the stairs. We laid him out flat on the floor, with a pillow for his head and the broken leg pulled straight as we could get it. The skin wasn't broken, no bones protruding, but you can never tell with a leg. It's better far to wait for the guys who can tell. They'd said they'd send an ambulance.

"I'm glad," I said to the kids, "that you guys were here."

Rick looked at me. I never could read him the way I flatter myself I can read most people. Emotionally, I had a feeling, the kid was in pain a lot, and he'd had plenty of practice hiding it. "Is it possible," he asked, "that the guy's a fink?"

I remembered Lassiter's funny smile when he talked about finding the body in the river, or not finding it. I remembered his tension—some people might call it hysteria—as the evening built, as I slipped out on him, when I told him what happened in Glenwood Canyon.

Would your killer get drunk with you? It wasn't a question I really wanted to answer.

"I hate to be the one to say it, but the truth is, anything's possible. You guys feel any different about my offer? Because it still stands."

I wished as much as I'd ever wished for anything besides Martha Ross that they'd take me up on it, that they'd get out of town, out of the country even. The situation was closing in on me sure as sunrise, and if an explosion was coming, I wanted to be sure it didn't damage any more innocent bystanders.

"That," said Charlie, "would be true finkery."

"It seems you're stuck with us, Joe." Rick laughed, and there was warmth in it.

The cowbell that hangs in an old iron bracket outside the front door rang twice. Two state troopers and a medic were there. I'd never seen any of them before. They didn't say much, refused my offer of drinks or coffee, went right to work on Lassiter. It was a break, just below the knee. The cops collected his luggage and gun, and I made my account of what happened as simple as I could. And with excuses for old Lassiter.

"It's an old house, Officer, it makes funny noises. He was a stranger. Maybe he thought he heard something." *Maybe he wanted to do a bit of target practice on Joe Birds' brain pan.*

He was laconic. "Maybe. We'll talk to him in the morning. I'll report to Richards, and no doubt Richards will want to talk to you all. And," he added, looking dubiously around at the pots, pans, and bottles that still lined windows and part of the staircase, "he'll get you a replacement."

"Thanks."

"Don't mention it."

He left as briskly as he'd come.

"That guy," said Charlie, chuckling into what was left of his beer, "thinks we are desperate characters."

We are. Anyway, one of us is.

"No doubt. Well. Shall we reset the trap, now that we know it works?"

"Why not?" Rick beamed as though he'd invented mountains. I could guess, without asking, that the booby-trapping had been his idea. We reset the traps and for the second time that night I backed my way upstairs. It was nearly four in the morning. Sunday morning. The bone-deep tiredness had slowly transformed itself into something else, a numb state beyond just exhaustion. But not quite numb enough to dull the sense of outrage that all this was still happening, and happening to me, and for no reason.

They didn't have to kill me, whoever they were. Whatever they were after, I didn't have it.

Rita was asleep, curled on her side like a child. I climbed into the bed gently as I could and lay for a while on my back, head resting on folded arms, watching the orange lights of the dying fire flick whiplashes of color on the ceiling.

Rita gave out a small, discontented sigh and shifted in her sleep. Far away, all the way across the valley probably, a big dog barked twice and shut up. The dying fire had a soft whispering language of its own, loud in the silent night, a hissing and settling, an occasional soft pop.

In some bleak Philadelphia cemetery, men would have spent the afternoon wrestling with the tight-frozen earth to make a place for the last of Blake Ross.

I wondered what graves were being dug for me.

Sleep was a long time coming.

Maybe you saw the Blake Ross funeral on television.

They have it down to a fine art now, adding dignity to the horror, gilding murder with grandeur: burying assassinated leaders has become an industry in America, a media event. Tell that to the bullet that blows your life away.

Martha had her wish. It was simple, as these things go, simple as you can be with three-network national television coverage, with speeches by everyone who's anyone or aspires to be anyone in politics, with a tribute from the president himself, with a funeral cortege bird-dogged by helicopters and two young girls badly trampled in the crush at Independence Hall after the second of the two memorial services, the first having been in the Capitol at Washington.

I already knew Blake Ross had been a very important man. The speeches added weight to that impression. The speakers of the speeches might have meant all the grand things they said, but even if they didn't, the bare fact that the speeches were made, and by these men, and in this tone of voice, meant something. Blake was dead, and safe dead, and now his fame was safe and would even grow, maybe grow taller than it would have in life.

A lot of the coverage was on Martha. Martha made no speeches, and any tears she wept were not for the cameras. But there she was, all through the two black days, a small, straight mourner at her husband's side, at the side of the huge stone sarcophagus as it lay in the Capitol Rotunda cold under its flag, sealed from the perfume of a million floral offerings, deaf to the footsteps of the shuffling crowds. And Martha was there in the back of the limousine with Blake's parents, first in a long, long line that crept out of Washington as if slowed by its weight of sorrow. She was at the service in Independence Hall, and of course at the graveside. The TV cameras were denied the burial itself, private, family only, but American know-how was not to be thwarted, and some enterprising newshound contrived to hover a few hundred feet overhead in a chopper whose clatter, she later told me, effectively drowned out the graveside prayers.

I slept late on Sunday.

No one woke me, and it was nearly eleven before I was up and dressed and made it down for a big lazy breakfast. It was a pretty day. The cut-crystal morning mountain sunlight danced and sparkled, and even a nighttime room like the bar at Joe's Place took on a certain jaunty optimism. The booby traps were gone. I might have dreamt them. Rita cooked me her special cornmeal waffles with plenty of sausages and a lake of maple syrup, and after three cups of Charlie's well-known, curl-your-hair coffee the day looked pretty good. Until I began thinking about the night before.

These thoughts were interrupted by the arrival, not unexpected, of Captain Richards. I shook his hand. Then I swiped a pot of coffee and an extra cup and led him upstairs.

"What happened?" He looked like he'd had a night of it, too.

"I was just about to ask you that. Have you talked to Lassiter?"

He had. "It seems he heard a noise."

"How much," I began, having decided that the time was long gone for pulling punches, "do you know about him?"

"He's straight, Joe. Been with us five years."

"If someone came creeping up your stairs at three in the morning, pistol drawn, what would you think?"

"I know. Look, you've gotta believe—"

"Captain, the less I believe, the more likely I am to be alive tomorrow. Your offer—of custody—is looking better and better by the minute. I'd probably take it, if I thought it'd work. Believe me, I am not a hero."

Or a martyr, either. Not for anybody's cause.

"Why do you think it won't work?"

"Because I'm just paranoid enough to think this really is some kind of a conspiracy. Meaning a big, fancy, well-financed, smart conspiracy. Just like all the crackpots claim about the Kennedy boys. And if I'm right—and I don't see anyone rushing to contradict me—those kinds of creeps might have people anywhere. Anywhere at all. Including, forgive me, in the state police."

Richards looked at me, then at his coffeecup, which needed filling. I filled it. He ran his big, squared-off forefinger around the rim of the cup slowly, deliberately, as though he expected it to chime like crystal. It didn't, it couldn't: if was half-inch-thick mottled brown earthenware made by a three-times-divorced millionairess with a ranch up Roaring Fork.

The moment of silence did nothing to cushion the tension between us.

"He's a local boy," Richards repeated slowly, as if educating the retards. "He's been with us for five years."

I know how he felt. He was being accused of harboring termites in his nice clean structure, and he didn't want to so much as admit that any termite ever had existed, anywhere.

"How long," I asked patiently, "was Brutus in the Roman Senate?"

This was not the tack to take with Richards, or anybody else. I kept feeling I was at the end of my rope, and it was fraying, and the only one to see the little deadly strands unraveling was me. I wanted to scream, stamp my feet, break things. Instead, I drank my coffee and poured both of us some more.

"Look," Richards said, summoning up a small extra measure of patience from a reservoir that must have been at the low-tide mark for several days now, "of course you're uptight about this. And, by George, we will look into that kid's background very damn close. Reliable, that's what he is, dead reliable. Maybe Lassiter won't set the world on fire, but sure as we're sitting here, he is honest."

I wished he hadn't used the word "dead."

"It's kind of pointless to talk about it, Captain. What shakes me up is, he was a lousy bodyguard. First he let me skip out on him, then this."

"The man you're getting instead," said Richards, as if reading from the Ten Commandments, "will not let you slip out on him. Or anyone slip in."

"I wouldn't have it any other way."

"Hank Wyland." Richards said that as though the name

was explanation enough in itself. He might have been saying "Captain Marvel."

"He couldn't be anything but an improvement."

"Fact is"—Richards chuckled—"that old Lassiter might really be happier at some desk job anyway. He'll get one now, that's sure as shootin'."

Dead reliable. Sure as shootin'. The geese were stampeding over my grave.

"When does he get here?"

"In about an hour." Richards looked at his watch, and I at mine. It was twelve-thirty. He shifted in his chair. "Tell me about the canyon."

I told him, slowly, putting in every detail I could remember, glad I'd told the story twice before in twenty-four hours. He nodded, sipped his coffee, and stayed silent. A good, trained listener. Only when I finished did he ask a few questions, smart questions, to-the-point questions. After maybe fifteen minutes he seemed satisfied.

"The Lincoln," he began quietly, "was stolen in Denver two weeks ago. There was no one in it when we pulled it out of the river this morning. No blood, no sign of anything, no fingerprints. In other words, Joe, a professional job."

"What about me?"

"What about you? You're an innocent young man that people are trying to kill, for reasons best known to themselves."

"But there was a guy in that car."

"You'll never prove it by me."

"Captain, they were here. I didn't dream them up. Or last night, either."

"Joe Bird, some of you college guys are just as thick as an old saddle. We are tryin' to help you, Joe. Officially, there was no one in that car. It was an accident, Joe. If we find the guy, which is not likely, considering the speed of the river and where it goes, but saying we do find the son of a bitch, how do we connect him with the damnfool stolen Lincoln? It's only your word and no proof, Joe Bird, and if I were you, I'd just pretend it was all a kind of a bad dream."

I didn't have to pretend very hard to pretend that.

"I'm sorry, Captain. I guess this is making me a little crazy."

Maybe more than a little.

"Hell and damn, Joe. Never think I don't know what it must be like. We may be just cops, and we may be a little slow . . ."

"You're not—"

He cut in on me then. "Let me say it. We have our Lassiters, that was a mistake, even though I do still swear he's an honest one, and we do know what a damn pickle you're in. Your man'll be here before you know it, Joe. And more than that, we've got three more, in shifts, and they're going to be watching this place from three different locations. And they're sharpshooters. I—just speaking personally now—happen to think you're not a bad sort. But even if you were the lowliest worm that ever crawled, we would be bending over ourselves to see that nobody and nothing gets to you, Joe. It's our job and it's our pride."

I deserved the lecture. My fuse has never been long enough, and every hour of the last few days had cut it shorter and shorter until there was just about nothing left of it at all. That showed, and it showed itself in rudeness and smart-ass remarks.

"I'm sorry if anything I said rubbed you the wrong way, Captain. You've got a fine force, and—"

"I know. We're just wonderful." He stood up then, but he stood up grinning. "I've got to get on now. Take it easy, Joe."

"I'll try." A smile found its way to my face, and for once it felt at home there.

"You'll like the new guy."

"Hank Wyland?"

"Hank Wyland."

I saw the captain out into the bright Aspen noon.

I stood in the doorway watching Richard's broad back move confidently across the narrow sidewalk to his car. The light dazzled my eyes, and my nose quivered to inhale the pure cold air. The air smells different when there's new snow. There's an edge to it, hard and unmistakable even though the snow itself has no scent at all, especially not here in Aspen at nine thousand feet plus, or at the top of the mountains three thousand feet higher. Maybe it's an interior smell, the spoor of anticipation. As I stood idly watching the big state-police cruiser move off, that hint of snow in the air became painful to me, because suddenly I realized it would be an act of courage simply to step out of my own door. This must be how prisoners feel when a bird flies by their window, not lifted by the beauty of it but stabbed by a sense of bottomless loss.

Still thinking these cheerful thoughts, I turned back into the bar and forced a grin.

I told the kids about Lassiter's replacement. Their attitude was like mine: we'd believe him when we saw him.

In the meantime, there was nothing much to do, and that is what we did. Not one of us in that bar could make ten cents as a fabricator of small talk, and we knew and liked each other too much to try. So we sat around, not saying much, not doing much, waiting. Rita did crosswords. Rick went skiing. Charlie sharpened the edges on his best and then his second-best skis. I wondered how far the Colorado River could drag a corpse in twenty-four hours.

Our first customer of Sunday afternoon was Hank Wyland, right on schedule at half-past one.

If you were setting out to build yourself a textbook opposite to poor old Lassiter, you could do worse than using Hank as a model.

Hank Wyland is the kind of young man they keep trying—and failing—to describe in western movies: tall and easy-moving, strong as rocks, but with a nice quiet sense of humor and a gentle way about him, especially in the company of ladies. It's the kind of gentle that comes from confidence.

He arrived in an unmarked Ford wagon with a ski rack, his own powder skis—The Ski, very fancy—Lange ski boots in Popsicle orange, wearing jeans and Frye boots and an old sweater that were, if anything, even rattier than what Rick and Charlie and I usually got ourselves up in. The gear was right, all of it. And the man who came with the gear looked right, too.

There is a kind of man who seems to grow only in the American West, craggy-faced with plenty of shoulders and a body like stretched wire: rangy is the word, and that's where Hank came from. His family had a big ranch north of Sun Valley, and he'd spent most of his childhood on horses and on skis. Hank's hair was the color of straw, and shaggy; eyes gray-blue and alert; smile wide and quick. We took to him instantly, it would have been hard not to.

Hank fit right into Joe's Place. He hadn't been with us an hour before I began to feel better about the day, the cops, and the future of civilization in general.

Sunday is never one of our busier days. It's a checking-in, checking-out day for the tourists, which keeps a lot of our ski-bum, hotel-clerk regulars busier than they usually are. A few people wandered in around three, including two Chicago reporters who found my "No comments" no more stimulating than the dozens of other reporters who had been darkening my door these last three days. It was nothing like a crowd, nothing that Charlie and Rita couldn't handle blindfolded.

Hank asked me if there was someplace we could talk.

We took some coffee upstairs, and settled in my living room. He looked around the room. "Nice."

"Thanks."

Hank sat himself in the leather wing chair, or, rather, he unfolded all six-three of himself into the chair, occupying it like a friendly army. I was glad he was there. I was glad there was so much of him. He drank a little coffee and looked at me over the rim of the big earthen cup.

"It's a bad one," said Hank Wyland, "very bad."

"We may never know just how bad it is."

"You've been here some time, Joe. You know the kinds of crimes we get—if we get any, which mostly we don't. We get some drunk rancher now and again, shooting his brother-in-law over poker. We get a few badass kids who think they're Billy the Kid. Now and then some drugs, meaning hard drugs—we aren't exactly breaking our asses on pot. But"—he paused to sip the coffee—"what we have here is a whole entire new breed of animal. It's tricky and it's complicated just as is. And it is more complicated because of who Blake Ross was and who he knew. When you're a simple local cop and you're dealing with world-famous types like Ross . . ."

"Or Austin Pierce?"

I wanted to try that on him, check the reaction. I hadn't been hearing anyone mention Pierce lately. And I wondered why.

"He's another one, sure. Pierce. Very highly connected, as they say. Meaning, we locals had better watch our asses, 'cause if we rub old Pierce the wrong way, Pierce or anyone like him, we may just wake up some fine day to discover we're directing traffic in beautiful downtown Denver."

"What do you make of it, Hank?"

"I think you took the wrong chair last Friday."

I actually laughed. "It has to be a conspiracy." My cup was empty. I put it on the table next to the sofa.

"Unless you buy the mad-sniper theory, which, believe it or not, has actually been suggested."

"By what half-wit?"

"I'd rather not say, 'cause he is one. Half-wit. One of ours, more's the pity. I think—since you're kind enough to ask—that it sure as hell is a conspiracy, and a fancy one. Know why?"

"I give up."

"Skiing. Your basic everyday thug does not ski. Mafiosi don't ski. Can you see Lee Harvey Oswald on skis? What we have here is a very . . . upscale kind of a conspiracy."

"Right-wing fanatics?"

"That would fit. Considering Blake Ross's politics. Which I don't know a whole lot about, but he's described as a liberal Democrat, which in certain circles is about the same as a flaming communist."

"The classic Kennedy-conspiracy theories all revolve around rich Texans." *And we have one among us, Hank, our own private rich Texan, complete with tricky eyes and two private planes and a plug-in to the Rosses and a house at Snowmass.*

"Sure. They make such nice fat targets."

"You don't buy that?"

"I'm not sure, Joe, not at all sure. How could I be? I'm just one of the cops on the beat. One thing you can be sure of is, we're getting plenty of help. FBI help. Maybe even CIA help. In fact, so many people are helping us, it'll be tough to pin down the blame when the case isn't solved."

"Why do they want to get me?"

"If we knew that . . ." Suddenly he stood up, stretched, stretched his long arms out, strained every tendon, a big outdoor man restless in his cage. My cage. "I have to think they think you know something. You claim you don't."

"It isn't a claim, Hank." *Hear that Martha? You asked me*

not to say anything, and I didn't. Will that buy me credits in hell, Martha?

He looked down at me from what seemed like an enormous height and grinned. "Of course it isn't. I only wish I knew how to convince your pal with the hunting bow, or your other pal with the stolen Lincoln about that."

"It has to be a conspiracy. There have to be a lot of them, and they have to be well-informed, and financed, and mobile. To learn the Rosses were coming out here. To pick a spot on Big Burn and just wait . . ."

"I know. Private knowledge versus public knowledge. Everybody knew Jack Kennedy was going to be in Dallas that day, and what he'd be riding in, and what the parade route was. This is more subtle."

The phone rang then. It was an operator in Philadelphia, wanting Rick. Operators in Philadelphia always wanted Rick, a lot more than he wanted them. I promised to give him the message.

I turned to Hank and shrugged. "Maybe," I said, "I ought to take an ad in the local papers, you know, 'To whom it may concern, Joe Bird doesn't know whatever you slimy murderers think he knows, so lay off, pick on someone your own size.' "

"I know the bullet went right through him," said Hank in a different tone of voice, more serious now, "but how soon did he die?"

"Like I said. I wasn't, God knows, timing the poor guy. Not five minutes."

"And he did say things?"

"Yes. He said: 'he did it,' and then he got off about two sentences. All about his wife."

Well, most of it was true. I haven't had a whole lot of practice at lying. I couldn't help wondering if it showed.

"Nothing that indicated he felt . . . threatened?"

"No. It was all private, and he broke off in mid-sentence and just . . . went under."

"You reported this to Mrs. Ross?"

"Sure. He asked me to. She was very moved, naturally, but she couldn't really make a whole lot of sense out of what he said. He said: 'Tell Martha to watch out . . .' and that was it. The first thing he said was . . . private."

"I see."

"So," I went on, "you understand how crazy it is for anyone to think I hold the key to some gruesome conspiracy. Or whatever it is."

"The world is a crazy, crazy place, Joe. We just have to make sure the craziness doesn't get any closer than it has already."

"Let's do that."

We went downstairs and I bought him a beer. And I very nearly told him about O'Leary. But I hadn't told Richards, so why tell Hank?

Joe's Place stayed Sunday-quiet through suppertime and all night long. And even though my head told me Sundays were never big nights at my place, there was another part of me that wanted to attribute this sense of peace to the arrival of Hank Wyland. I wanted Hank to be Captain Marvel, to ward off the bad guys, to solve problems and make everything come out all right in the end. I needed to think he could do these things, needed the thought like a drug, because I had long since stopped dreaming I could do anything much about it myself. Last night in the canyon had been like a bad dream, just the way Richards said it was.

We all had steaks and salad and red wine.

After the meal Hank borrowed Rita's Spanish guitar and sang for us. He sang easily, as he seemed to do everything, naturally, floating into the old Western trail songs in which lonesome cowboys bemoaned the gals they'd left behind them and told about prairies empty in the moonlight and Indian raids and cattle drives and gold in the high sierras and impossible loves for sequestered Mexican beauties. There is something curiously medieval in these ballads, maybe in all ballads, and Hank's easy, dry, country-boy voice fitted them beautifully. He was every brokenhearted troubadour in all the songbooks of the world. It did us all good to watch Hank Wyland, me especially.

He might be helping Charlie tend bar—which Hank did expertly—or stroking the guitar and singing, but at no time was he missing a trick.

You never got the impression of a man on the alert, but here was as alert a man as I'd ever seen. It seemed to come naturally to him, the way smiles came naturally to his long bony face, the way songs came floating up naturally from some deep well of music inside him. Hank made me feel safe again. Maybe that was dangerous, but for me, at least, it was also necessary. Too much had been coming at me, too fast, and too deadly. I didn't feel up to any new challenges, new puzzles, new violence.

Rick wandered back around ten and got on the horn to Philadelphia. He came away from the phone with a worried expression, typical result of his calls back East. His family, it seemed, were trying everything this side of outright kidnapping to get him back into their mold. It must have been a tight, uncomfortable little mold, because Rick was a good kid and nothing like a troublemaker. Just troubled. He cheered up after a few minutes of talking to Hank Wyland. Hank seemed to have that effect on people, on my people anyway.

Before long they were giving us country-music duets, Hank on guitar, both of them singing. I'd never heard Rick sing before. He had a light, clear tenor that contrasted nicely with Hank's deeper twang.

We kidded around like that until nearly midnight, then decided to close early. Rick and Charlie and Hank reset the booby traps, which Hank thought were a fine idea.

"You will definitely not"—he laughed—"find old Hank stumbling up those stairs with a loaded six-shooter. Hell, that Lassiter like to have shot himself sooner'n anybody else."

We all had a good laugh about that and went peacefully to bed.

9

I woke early in an empty bed still warm from where Rita must have just gotten out of it. For a few delicious moments I just lay there with my eyes closed and the lightweight down comforter pulled up to my chin doing its job, comforting me. I could use all the comfort available. Even with my eyes closed I could tell we'd had new snow that night.

There is a special silence that only the insulation of a few inches of new powder can give to a whole valley, an entire mountain, all of a skier's world. That silence was in my room, seeping in from the town, floating down the slopes of old Ajax Mountain, drifting along the valley, finding its way up the miniature canyon cut by the Roaring Fork River.

A car went by outside, the sound of its motor muffled almost before it reached my window. A door slammed down the street, slammed with no echo.

It was going to be a very quiet Monday in Aspen, Colorado.

I wiggled my toes. They lusted after my ski boots. I stretched my legs. Except for a spot of rock-throwing, which you could hardly count as true exercise, I'd been a very cooped-up, indoor kind of guy these last few days. My eyes were still closed. I smiled to myself, a naughty kid contemplating hooky. Hank Wyland had, after all, brought his skis. They couldn't be for decoration.

Maybe. Just maybe . . .

The subject would have to be approached with the greatest delicacy. After all, Hank was my legal guardian. His job was to keep me bulletproof.

And we all knew what could happen on chair lifts.

Still and all, it was a new week in Aspen, fresh-minted and

with new snow on the hill. It was a day that screamed to be skied. It didn't have to scream very loud for me to hear.

I asked him straight out, over breakfast. He looked at me, then grinned. "I thought you'd never ask. I think it'll be safe enough, Joe. I am one of the few members of the force who agrees with your living as normal a life as you can. Under the circumstances. And, like they say, a moving target . . ."

"Beats a sitting duck?"

"We can hope so. How's about a few runs down Ajax, crisscrossing trails, unpredictable skiing. Whoever set up Blake Ross knew you can't ski Snowmass without at least trying the Burn."

"You don't have to twist my arm."

We all went. The pressures had been building in every one of us, each in different ways, and it was like a holiday from school, only better. There was the usual small scramble while we located boots, gloves, parkas, goggles. Some instinct had made all of us get up a little early, so it was still only a hair after nine when we locked up Joe's Place and trudged off to catch one of the first rides of the day up the number-one lift on Ajax Mountain, which conveniently begins about three blocks from my door.

It was a postcard day, the kind of day that looks retouched when you see it reproduced on paper: sky more blue than sapphires, snow deep and dazzling, and everything and everyone standing out with a special clarity that simply does not exist at sea level.

We set off, the five of us, in a circus-going, hooky-playing mood.

Rick taped a sign to the front door of Joe's Place that read: "CATCH US IF YOU CAN!"

Maybe it was a little juvenile, taking it this lightly. But that was how we felt, us against the forces of evil, whoever they were. You can feel grim for only so long, especially in Aspen, especially on a day like that Monday.

Hank and I got on the chair lift together.

"Okay, copper, if you were the bad guys, where would you lurk?" Joking and not joking: I really wondered. The slats of the chair pressed into my back as we were lifted off the loading platform and I felt the old vulnerability again, just a few sticks and a lot of air between me and—who knew what?

"Well, Joe. They're schemers and plotters, and maybe not all that bright, at least on the bottom rung. The dirty-work level, so to speak. If they were really smart, they wouldn't have tried to chase a Porsche with a Lincoln. Both times they've tried something on you, it's been a setup, just like the Ross killing was a setup. Since they couldn't have known we'd be damnfools enough to go skiing, they couldn't very well set us up, now, could they? At least, that's what I'm banking on."

If Hank was banking on a thing, I'd bank right along with him.

The chair swept us relentlessly into the bright blue morning.

For a while we said nothing, just sat back and let the day happen. That was good therapy too. Far overhead a big golden eagle made slow, watchful circles, his wings touched with gold, moving to his own music, gliding with never a flick of those great wings, riding the roofless sky in stately silence, with the casual insolence of kings and princes. The bird had a sinister kind of beauty. It made me think of death and angels. Another thing about Eagle Grove: there were no eagles anymore.

The chair lift that was taking me up Ajax Mountain was taking me not one inch closer to finding out things like where O'Leary really was, and what he really knew, and why Blake Ross mentioned him, dying. Maybe sometime I could ask Hank for an opinion. Maybe.

We got off the number-one chair and backtracked diagonally across the mountain over the bottom of a trail named Silver Queen after one of the old mines, then skied down the top of Little Nell to the base of number-five lift, which would take us up the middle third of the big mountain. The number-five lift line was short, and if there were any killers lurking, they were lurking well enough to be invisible.

I still had that uncomfortable feeling of being trapped every time the chair came swinging around to lift us up the hill.

Hank was first to break the silence. "I wish," he began, "that I knew more about politics."

"You mean, who profits by Blake's death?"

"If it was political profit, yes."

"What else would it be, a guy like that?"

Hank looked at me, then past me, frowned a slow cowboy frown, scanning the horizon for rustlers. Or killers.

"We tend to think it's an assassination. But we don't really know that. Almost all plain everyday murders are crimes of passion, done by friends or relatives. Usually lovers. Suppose there's a woman scorned, as they say, or a jealous husband . . . who knows?"

Certainly not me. "He had a pretty public life, to be fooling around."

"Once," said Hank thoughtfully, "there was a man called Jack Kennedy. There was a lady called Judith Campbell. And all the other ladies. Including one they found dead."

I thought of Blake, and the way he looked, the charisma. Girls would have fallen out of trees on him. The thought of Blake always came neatly wrapped in thoughts of Martha. Beautiful Martha. The lovely Mrs. Blake Ross. Maybe she was lovely enough for someone to want her to be a widow. I shuddered then. The day was too beautiful for thoughts like these. Suddenly we were unloading at the top of number-five lift.

It's another little commuter run from the top of number five down to the base of number three, which takes you all the way to the top. Three lift is shorter, steeper, and it gets you there faster. In all, when we eased off three, we'd spent the better part of an hour just getting up Ajax.

It was time well spent.

The morning stretched out below us, filled with sunshine and possibilities. There were about six inches of new powder on a packed base, and being more than eleven thousand feet up was only one reason it looked like heaven.

Charlie was last off the chair lift. He came swooping up to us and said one word: "Gentleman's!"

He didn't get any arguments. Gentleman's Ridge is a long black-diamond trail that skirts the far-right side of Ajax in a steep, sweeping series of dips and curves. It was a good choice. Black diamond equals "Experts Only" in the new, kinder psychology of ski-trail nomenclature, and the chances were it'd be relatively unskied. And relatively free of killers.

Down we went, starting with North Star, which melds into the ridge about a third of the way down. Charlie took the lead, as usual, all stops out, clowning and yodeling, moving with the instinctive grace of a world-class skier. Charlie was too much in love with the fun of skiing to discipline himself into a racer, but he had all the raw ingredients handy and he wasn't afraid to use them. It was a pleasure to watch the kid, and a little eerie too: he reminded me of myself fifteen or so years ago.

The rest of us kept in fairly close order, Rita and Hank and Rick and me, moving right along but not straining for speed, gliding across the trail and recrossing it, carving a pattern of braided ski trails deep in the new snow, flickering in sun dappled by the blue grid of shadows cast from big Colorado spruce trees, building a kind of rapture self-contained but silently shared too, an interior joy made of equal parts speed and beauty whose only background music is the hiss of honed-steel ski edges cutting thoughtless arabesques in snow whiter than any marble.

There was no doubt about it: Hank Wyland could ski.

We took Gentleman's Ridge in three long runs, stopping just for breath and saying very little until the trail unfolded itself into Jackpot Bowl and then wound down a beginner's trail to the base of number five again.

"Not bad," said Hank, grinning, as we slipped into the lift line. "In fact, very good. On skis, Mr. Bird, you are a very moving target."

"You move pretty good yourself, Hank, considering you're fuzz and all."

He laughed, and the chair came around again, too suddenly, and before we knew it we were airborne again and hanging like two sides of beef from this giant meathook in the sky.

I was ready this time when the fear came. That didn't stop it from coming, but it made me feel a little better able to handle it, to step on it before it grew into something unmanageable, to send it cringing and snarling back into whatever small cage it lived in, somewhere back in my alleged brain.

"Who," I asked him, "is actually running this investigation? I mean, is it you guys, or Billy Medina, or the feds?"

I didn't expect the loudness of Hank's laughter. "I know," he said, still laughing, "this is anything but a laughing matter. But the answer is, all of the above. I'm afraid we've got ourselves more tails than dogs, all wagging to the beat the band.

Everyone's in charge. Your Medina is in charge locally. Richards for the state. And I don't know who for the feds. And we are told the CIA may be poking around somewhere."

"Isn't there some kind of a pecking order?"

"There always is. But this is subtle, Joe, and you've gotta remember, I'm just a simple country boy and I stay out of the political parts."

Sure.

"And there are political parts?"

"Publicly and privately, only, who's going to admit it? There's always a kind of interservice rivalry, keep your act off my street corner, buddy—that kind of thing. Who does the dirty work, who gets the credit. This is a very complicated situation, and it's going to get more complicated before it clears up."

"You think it will clear up?"

Hank looked at me, put his hand on my arm. "I have to think that. So do you."

"You're the doctor."

And I was the patient. And I did feel better, not for any logical reason except the fact of Hank's being there.

The chair lift let us off at the top of Deer Park, and we could have come down any of six ways. What we did was run the connecting trail to the bottom of Deer Park and across Spar Gulch to the little connecting chair lift, number six, which quickly took us across the face of Ajax to the far right of the mountain, to the top of Ruthie's Run, my other favorite trail after Gentleman's Ridge.

Ruthie's is the Powderhorn of Ajax, a great wide richly moguled sweep of a run with its own private chair lift. It was getting on past eleven when we reached the top of Ruthie's, and Hank suggested this be our final run. We'd been out of phone's reach for nearly three hours now, he said, and that was enough. I told the kids to stay all day if they liked, but they weren't buying that, good soldiers all.

We stood together at the top of the trail in a disordered row, a motley army but a happy one, five of us against the hill, against who-knew-what-else.

This time I led the way down.

If you're me, you start off skating a little, which is an unnecessary gesture left over from days of racing. Unnecessary because the mountain makes you its gift of speed soon enough and the deep irresistible logic that takes charge of all falling objects gets to work for you or against you, depending on how you play it.

These days I play it fairly cool, entering into a kind of bargain with the hill, patiently resisting the temptation to damn-all start flying, which is a very seductive possibility always hanging out there just beyond your ski tips. The mountain takes over then with its rush of air and the gentle violence of eternal rock upholstered with transient snow that comes on soft but can snap bones like matchsticks if you don't work the hill right, but you do work it right, at least most of the time, if you're still alive and gliding after all those years, all those mountains. You get the easy rhythms in the turns and you ride the fall line like a thing on tracks and the long slim knife-steel edges underneath you carve a special private message in the singing plumes of powder and that message is now, simple and forever: that you are free in this instant of time, as few things in the shopworn world ever are free, and only you and the mountain know your fate and for one quick shimmering moment you have yourself convinced it could be like this always, always beautiful, wishes borne on wind, gliding, soaring, and forever. It is a drug, a passion, a folly.

But all trails end, and even mountains have their roots in flat earth.

"Man, you were really moving there." Charlie swept up beside me where I'd stopped in the runoff, and we stood there together, flushed and breathing puffs of white vapor, watching the others finish their run, three dark specks dancing down the whiteness and quickly enlarging into Rita and Hank and Rick. Rick was skiing slowly today, not his usual self. They pulled up beside us.

"Where's the fire?" Hank laughed.

"Well," I said, sharing the laugh, "it was like this, Officer, help, the paranoids are after me, as they say on the button."

"They," said Hank, "would have to be pretty damn fast paranoids: the way you took off, I thought something really was chasing you."

"You never know."

We cruised down to the runoff, taking it easy, squeezing every last ounce of pleasure from the golden morning, not wanting to touch ground, not wanting it ever to end. We took our skis off and walked back to Joe's Place, saying little, cherishing the magic of the morning.

I looked at my house with a stranger's eyes, with the eyes of a murderer. It needed paint.

How would I attack Joe's Place? Fire at night? A grenade through the bedroom window? A sniper's bullet? These cheerful thoughts raced through my head, and maybe through Hank's and the kids' heads too, to judge by their silence. Not to mention the head of person-or-persons-unknown, the charming folks who had nominated me as clay pigeon of the year.

The sun sparkled off my windows and did nothing to cheer me up. Rick's cardboard sign fluttered a little in the gentle valley breeze: "CATCH US IF YOU CAN!"—a taunt, an act of defiance no less gallant for being hollow. If you can. Well, they hadn't. Yet.

We went inside and packed our gear away. Hank climbed upstairs to make a few phone calls. Soon the air was filled with cheeseburgers grilling and our mugs were filled with Coors beer and I just about forgot that I should have been worrying over what was going to become of Martha Ross, and what was going to become of me.

Hank came downstairs with the faintly distracted air of someone who has a few too many choices in front of him. I suppose he did. Hank favored coffee over beer. He sat down. "No news."

"Is that good news?" Rita served us Aspen's finest cheeseburgers on sourdough bread toasted golden.

"Not," said Hank, "as far as I'm concerned. They're still looking for that damned bullet up on Snowmass, and for the gun, and the more they look, the more sure I get they'll never find 'em. Not unless we really are dealing with a bunch of amateurs."

"How long," asked Rick, "does an investigation continue, if they don't find anything? I mean, isn't there a cutoff point, a time when they just throw in the towel?"

It was a good question, and I didn't want to know the answer.

"You'll never hear it officially, especially not from me," said Hank quietly, "but, sure there's a cutoff. Not standard, mind, but depending on the nature of the case. It's scary how many crimes of all kinds go unsolved just because we haven't got the time or the staff or the money to keep people on the job full-time. This mess," he said gently, looking at me with something that might have been sadness or pity, "will have a much longer run than the exact same thing if it happened to Joe Blow."

"It's a great feeling." Rick stood up and glared at Hank as though Hank was the author of our troubles. A lot of the things Rick had been bottling up these last three days came pouring out. "Here we sit, trapped like—"

"Rats?" Hank's question had an edge of mockery to it. He wasn't about to take crap from children. I couldn't blame him. Or Rick either.

"Yes, dammit," Rick went on in a low voice that had plenty of carrying power all the same, "like rats. I know it isn't your fault, Hank, but isn't there anything—?"

"Sure there is. We could all go home and pretend it never happened. Leastways, you could. Everybody could, but Joe here. And he could always change his name, grow a beard, and move out."

I laughed then, but not because I felt like laughing.

"That," said Rick testily, "is hardly what I meant." When Rick got upset, he reverted to type, and the type was purebred Eastern Establishment, every flag flying, all self-assurance and scorn. It didn't make a pretty picture: Rick was better than that, and most of the time he knew it.

"Rick. Look." Hank smiled his big easy smile, and the scene began to change direction, because this was real confidence, genuine ease, authentic control. "I know what you mean, how you feel. We all feel it. We all feel like going right out and tearing the bastards limb from limb. And maybe one day we will. Meanwhile, there's this little matter of finding out who the bastards are. And also, protecting ourselves as much as we can. Everything that can be done is being done. There's something like a total of twenty-seven good men on the case right now, here and in Washington and in Philadelphia. I truly think we will get 'em. It's the waiting that's the hard part. Always has been. Always is."

"Yeah." Rick sat down again and finished his cheeseburger. "But isn't there anything more we can do?"

"Only to be alert, which you are. And not to let this one"—he touched my shoulder—"take chances."

"Well I still—"

"We all do, Rick." Rita spoke softly too, like Hank, but her words sliced through the tension.

"What we really need to do," I said, laughing, trying maybe a little too hard to make a joke of it, "is have some more beers. How about it, bartender?"

Rick got up smiling and drew everybody a beer. "They'll find us," he said, pouring, "in the spring, safe as houses, drunk as skunks."

"It eases the pain," I said.

The mood was lighter now. We relaxed with the cool beer. The phone rang. It was for Charlie. After a certain amount of murmuring and mumbling, a sure sign Charlie was talking to one of his girls, he hung up and came bashfully over to where I was sitting.

"You wouldn't," he asked, "happen not to be using the Porsche for a couple of hours?" That was standard. Rick had an old Chevy pickup, which he was generous in lending, but it was in the shop that day. "It seems," Charlie went on, "there's a lady who needs my services."

A lot of ladies needed Charlie's services.

"Sure." I tossed him the keys. "Have fun."

Rita went upstairs. Rick and Hank and I sat around the corner table toying with our beers, not saying much, reliving the morning.

I was conducting a great silent debate with myself on the burning question of whether to have another Coors when the explosion came.

10

It burst on us like thunder, one loud roar followed by the tinkle of glass breaking. One roar and silence. One roar from the back of Joe's Place, from the parking lot. From the lot where I kept the Porsche.

We all ran for the door. Hank got there first by a narrow margin.

The last thing I saw as I ran past the bar was Rick's sign. "CATCH US IF YOU CAN!"

Charlie was alive, but only barely.

The Porsche was a burnt, ruined thing, its driver's door blown awry, the glass all broken, the slick enamel black, smoking. Charlie sprawled on the ground. The parts of him that weren't scorched black were bloody. Hank probably saved the boy's life. Instantly, not stopping for the stench of burnt flesh, the risk of exploding gasoline, or sheer shock, Hank grabbed Charlie by the underarms and dragged him across the lot to the steps of my house. It was then that I noticed the mangled mess where Charlie's right foot had been.

Charlie, who lived for skiing. Charlie, who could have been me in that driver's seat, stepping on the accelerator, stepping on a bomb.

Hank whipped off his belt and made a rough tourniquet around Charlie's right thigh. A crowd was gathering.

Rita came out, took one look, and went back for blankets. I called the cops. We didn't dare move him more than we had, so we covered Charlie with three blankets, wiped his face with a damp cloth, and waited. We didn't wait long. You could hear the siren long before the ambulance got there, starting from the hospital far on the other end of the valley. I've never been religious. But then I prayed, hearing the wailing ambulance getting closer, prayed to a dozen gods, old ones, new ones, prayed then and prayed later. There was nothing else to do. No sound came from Charlie. We couldn't even hear him breathing. He was deep in shock, deeply unconscious, and only that was a kind of comfort to us, knowing he probably couldn't feel anything, knowing the moment of horror hadn't come for Charlie yet, the moment when he found out he was an amputee.

I rode with him in the ambulance.

The ride was less than ten minutes. It might have been a year. They wouldn't let me touch him. I sat crouched in the little jump seat looking at Charlie, waiting, hoping for any sign of life. And praying. Still he was silent, barely breathing, slipping away from us.

We raced past Ajax Mountain. I thought of the morning, of Charlie leading us down Gentleman's Ridge, Charlie brave in the new powder, yelping with pure puppy-dog joy, radiating life, Charlie who wouldn't know how to do an unkind thing, who gave nothing but pleasure. I wondered what girl was waiting for a date that might never be kept.

They wouldn't let me be with him in the emergency room.

Hank and Rita and Rick chased the ambulance in Hank's wagon. We all sat in the little waiting room, in the pleasant little hospital that usually dealt with nothing more serious than a broken ankle or a touch of frostbite. Maybe I'll live to see a longer hour than the one we spent waiting at the hospital. I hope not. The hospital staff was too busy trying to save Charlie's life, what was left of it, to feed us information, so there we sat in our own kind of shock, together, Rita and Hank and Rick and me, together but really each alone with horrors too deep and private to share.

My grief was amplified by a bottomless, uncontrollable sense of guilt: it should have been me.

Hank at least had a job to do. He found the phone and got working on it, although the local cops would already be on the scene. He went out into the hall to make his calls, and there were several of them. Once he was paged in the waiting room. The hour crept by.

Finally a doctor I didn't know came out and asked for me. "He'll make it. It's a damn lucky thing he was wearing a down parka: that helped protect the torso."

"What about the foot?"

"It's bad. An ugly wound. But it won't be a complete amputation. He's going to lose his toes, maybe a little more. But he'll be able to walk. What we're worried about is the inner ear. A blast like that can leave someone deaf, or worse."

"Brain damage?"

"It's a possibility. He'll get all the tests. And he'll be with us for at least a month. You'll want to get in touch with his family."

"Of course. What can we do for him right now?"

"Not a thing. He's sedated and he'll stay sedated at least until tomorrow morning. You can see him then. Meanwhile, I'd suggest you get some rest, get in touch with his family. Tell them he'll be all right. That he's had a close call. About the foot. They might want to come out here."

"I'll do that. And thanks."

We left then. I didn't know much about Charlie's family. His father was a stockbroker in San Francisco. Charlie never mentioned them when he could avoid it. I gathered all was not well at home, but how or why was a mystery.

We drove home in Hank's wagon. I began building a new life for Charlie in my imagination, wondering what a kid would do whose whole life had revolved around skiing, who'd now be at least partly crippled. Of course, he'd be able to ski, to do something like skiing. Even people who'd lost complete legs could ski, sort of, with those special ski poles fitted with a tiny ski instead of a spike and a basket at the tip. But would it be enough?

Hank had been very quiet ever since the explosion. We parked the wagon and went into Joe's Place and had a cup of coffee.

"You might want," he said softly, "to reconsider protective custody. The game's getting rougher."

The game has always been rough, Hank: ask Blake Ross. "The scariest thing about it all is that it's so completely unnecessary. I threaten no one."

"That," said Hank with a small flickering smile, "seems to be a matter of opinion."

The phone rang. I picked it up.

"Joe Bird?"

It was Austin Pierce.

"Speaking."

"Austin Pierce here, Joe. Martha asked me to call."

The polished voice flowed across the crackling wires and sounded distant at first, then closer. The electronic sounds on the line made a new doubt filter into my head: were they bugging the phone?

"How is she?"

"She's a brave little lady, Joe. Blake would have been proud of her. I'm afraid these next few weeks aren't going to be easy for poor Martha."

They weren't going to be easy for poor Joe, either, but that wasn't her fault. *"Tell Martha to watch her uncle . . ."* I didn't even know where Pierce was calling from, let alone how to go about watching him. I couldn't watch myself properly, even with the help of a professional keeper. Sorry about that, Blake, I'm letting you down, and I don't know what to do about it.

"Can I help, Austin?"

"That's very kind of you, Joe. To tell the truth, that's why I'm calling. You see, she's coming back."

Thanks, Martha. That's just what I need. "To Aspen?" I wondered if I sounded as dumb as I felt.

"To my house. I tried to dissuade her, Joe, because . . . well, you understand, the memories can't be . . . terribly pleasant for her."

Right on, Austin. Pleasant they most surely were not. "Why in the world would she want to come here?"

"Exactly my feeling, Joe. I suggested the ranch, or our little place in Lyford Cay, anyplace but here. . . ."

"You're at Snowmass now?"

"Yes. I flew in this afternoon, straight from the funeral. Martha's coming tomorrow afternoon."

If Pierce flew in this afternoon, after a big public funeral, then he had an alibi for the morning's bomb planting. If it had been done in the morning. It might as well have been done last night. Night would have been easier. And it was doubtful that Uncle Austin did his own dirty work in any case. He didn't strike me as the kind of man who'd want dirt, much less blood, on those soft pink hands.

"Listen, Joe," he went on, "I wonder if we could get together, perhaps tomorrow morning, and talk about this?"

"About Martha? Sure. Anytime."

"That's fine, Joe. Why don't I drop by, say, about ten? We'll have a good chat."

What did he want? What did he think I could give him, that he'd seek me out like this?

"Sure."

"Around ten, then."

"I'll be here."

"Fine."

The phone clicked off. So Austin Pierce and Joe Bird were going to have a nice cozy chat. I hoped Hank would be there to observe. Murder, I thought, as I went to look up Charlie's home phone number, makes strange bedfellows.

Charlie's parents were in Japan for a month.

When I set up Joe's Place, my lawyer advised me to incorporate. The corporation has a good health plan. Charlie would be taken care of as far as the medical bills were concerned. Who would take care of his head and his future? We all talked about that for a while, but there wasn't much point in talking until the kid could speak for himself.

We got through the rest of the evening somehow, and the night. Every time I looked at the empty place behind my bar, I saw Charlie, and every time I saw Charlie, I saw the way he looked sprawled on the parking lot next to the wreck of my car.

They'd taken what was left of the Porsche away for various kinds of analysis. A demolition expert was being flown in from Denver. No one in Aspen had experience with this kind of thing.

With Charlie gone, there was more work for me to do, and I did it gratefully, mechanically. Therapy. There wasn't much of a crowd. Apparently the novelty of murder attempts on Joe Bird was wearing thin. The reporters had given up on me after hearing one "No comment" too many. Some pals of Charlie's dropped in and we told them what news there was.

Once during that long night I found myself looking around the big old barroom with an appraiser's eye, wondering just how much I could get for the whole place, cash on the barrelhead. Cut and run. There are other good ski towns. My world doesn't really begin and end in Aspen. I could make do with Sun Valley or Alta or Snowbird.

We were quiet as we closed up for the night. Whatever Hank was thinking, he kept to himself. Rita and Rick were normally fairly quiet, at least in public. I could feel the trap I was in closing in on them now, just the way it had closed in on Charlie. We all must have been figuring the odds for and against making it alive and in one piece through the next few days. Figuring odds against silent phantoms, nameless, faceless beings who struck to kill.

It felt good to get to bed, but not even fatigue or a few glasses of wine or worrying could put me to sleep. I kissed Rita good night, too beat for love, and lay silent on my back listening to the familiar quiet rhythms of a ski town at two A.M. tucking itself into bed.

Whatever else I might have to face tomorrow, the worst of it would be facing Charlie. My mind riffled through a dozen versions of that scene, all of them bad. I found myself thinking, if the kid had died, then at least I wouldn't have to face him, or see the look in his eyes when I told him about the foot. I thought that, and hated myself for thinking it, and took it as a measure of what was happening to my brain. When the Visigoths finally made it through the gates, they rampaged well and truly. And in my head right then were Visigoths and Huns, monsters, Harpies, banshees in more sizes, shapes, and colors than Hieronymus Bosch ever thought of in his darkest hour, all dancing, all jabbing away with an arsenal of freshly sharpened pikes, swords, and axes. It wasn't what you'd call fun.

Tuesday dawned bright as a politician's promise. I got up early but not refreshed. Sleep had finally come to me, not a good sleep or a long one, but maybe better than nothing.

At nine o'clock I called the hospital to be told Charlie was still under, but gaining strength. We could see him in the afternoon. Reprieve.

Then something like a good idea seeped into the numbness inside my head. It would be about eleven o'clock in Washington, D.C. Blake Ross had an office. The office had a staff. The staff would have O'Leary's address. And phone number. Maybe O'Leary would even be in the office himself, right now, brimming with hot clues. I dialed 202 and the information number and in two minutes the Ross office gave me Robert O'Leary's home number in Arlington.

A woman answered. Either she had a cold or she smoked too much. Her voice was all sandpaper and gasping.

"Yes?"

"I wonder if I could speak to Mr. Robert O'Leary?"

Her laugh had long been drained of humor, and now it sounded like the devil sandpapering a sob. "That's not funny."

"Is this Mr. O'Leary's number?"

She was drunk, or crazy, or both. My words came back to mock me, moving through the coarse filter of her pain.

"Is this Mr. O'Leary's number?" Her voice reached a cackle, the mockery of a Walt Disney witch. "Oh, yes. Yes. This is Mr. O'Leary's number. They've got his number, all right. Haven't you heard?" The cackling trailed off now, and for a long beat there was silence. Then the rasping. "Mr. O'Leary is unavailable, sir."

"Do you know where I can reach him?"

Again, the mad laugh. "Yes. Yes, I do. I do know that. He has a new address in Arlington now. Pretty place, very well kept. You can see old Robert Lee's house on the hill. Mr. O'Leary is dead, young man. Dead. Dead. Unavailably dead."

I tried to tell her I was sorry, but the voice trailed off and there was a loud click as she hung up.

Robert O'Leary, dead. The paranoid's self-fulfilling prophecy had come true. How dead? Dead by accident? People died every day, of natural causes sometimes. And what could I do about it, without sounding even more paranoid than Martha had thought O'Leary was, with his conspiracy theories?

I wondered what she'd say when I told her this.

I was on my third cup of coffee when the cowbell rang. Ten A.M. precisely.

"I thought," said Austin Pierce affably as he sat with Hank and me over coffee, "that we might go for a little ride. In my plane. If that's all right with you, Officer Wyland."

"Reckon that'll be safe enough, Joe. Far as we know, they don't yet have antiaircraft weapons. Anyway"—he stood up—"the captain wants me in for some sort of war conference. Probably take all the morning."

"We'll be back no later than one." Pierce leaned back in the scruffy old chair, casually dressed but not casual. He looked out of place, and knew it, and was trying to compensate. His manner was fake-easy, just one of the boys. The boys that Austin Pierce was truly one of, tended to have many oil wells and all the trappings of big money and heavy influence. They definitely did not include Joe Bird, or anyone like him. "Mrs. Ross," he continued, "is coming in on the one-fifteen from Denver."

"I'll get my coat."

The door was an obstacle now. I had to psych myself up before walking through it into the too-perfect Aspen morning. Now when I saw clear skies and sunshine my first thought was what they'd do for a sniper's aim. Sunset was a threat now, because who knew what might be slinking around in the darkness. And I longed with a quick, sharp longing for the heartbreaking innocence of household pets and small children, for the blissful ignorance I'd known myself less than one week past.

"Charming place you have here," said Pierce as we walked toward the door. "Tremendously authentic-looking."

"I guess you could say it's kind of undecorated."

"Charming."

Pierce had a big white Ford wagon and he drove with an imperial disregard for all laws of man and gravity. I thought of my brutalized Porsche and made a note to rent a car. And I wondered if my insurance covered murder attempts.

We were at Pierce's private hangar in ten minutes.

"The little jet," he said apologetically, "is in Kansas City being overhauled."

We had to make do with his bloodred twin-engine Cessna. I helped him push it out of the hangar and onto the runway. I hoped his flying would turn out to be less dramatic than his driving.

His flight check was standard and complete. It gave me a chance to get a good look at his plane. Here was about a hundred thousand dollars' worth of highly customized Cessna. Inside the cockpit everything that could be padded was upholstered in rich tan cowhide branded here and there with a curiously joined scroll monogram "AP" which turned out to be his official cattle brand. The hides, naturally, were from Pierce cattle, just as the plane itself had been bought with money that flowed from Pierce oil wells. It was enough to make you wonder just how much he might have to lose from a piece of regulatory legislation likc the Ross/Tilden bill.

The instrument panel was padded in the same cowhide, and the knobs and dials and switches were set in highly polished brass that looked enough like gold to really be gold, and maybe it was. He got his clearance from the control tower and we taxied to the far end of the runway, easily maneuvering the solid, smooth-riding aircraft in the general direction of Aspen.

You take off pointing toward Snowmass, and for a time the runway runs parallel to and a little below Route 82 out of Aspen.

Just as we got airborne I noticed a state-police car speeding in the direction of Snowmass, or maybe toward Glenwood Canyon, which lies beyond. And I wondered if Hank Wyland was in that car.

"What a day! We've got VFR from here to Tacoma." Austin Pierce beamed like a department-store Santa Claus: just a little too brightly.

"What," I asked, "is VFR?"

"Visual Flight Rules. You don't need instruments. Naturally," he said, looking at me confidentially, one expert to another, "I use 'em anyway."

"Of course."

He banked the plane right and climbed fast and steady, then gently circled left toward Snowmass.

The whole clean new plan of the Snowmass area lay a few thousand feet below us, looking as fresh and crisp and unreal as the day someone put it all down on blueprints. The red plane climbed over the ski slopes and past the great stone sprawl of the Pierce house, which looked happy and rich and remote astride the blazing white mountain sprinkled with colorful skiers.

Only the steady, throaty growl of two perfectly tuned engines underlined the silence. We climbed and climbed, gliding over the big terraced restaurant on top of Sam's Knob and then banking left a little to survey Big Burn, which was in full-scale activity again after having been closed for three days to help the fuzz search for the bullet.

Why had he brought me up here?

Austin Pierce handled his plane easily, reflexively, with a sure physical instinct I wouldn't have guessed at, judging by all the soft, polished surfaces he presented to the world. He was quiet, but there was no sense of strain in the cockpit. We had all the time in the world. Or at least he made it seem that way.

He wants something from me.

"I see," I said aimlessly, "that they've opened the Burn again. Not a good sign."

"Why is that?"

"They must have given up on the bullet."

"I believe they are still searching, Joe. But in all fairness to the corporation, they were losing thousands of dollars every day they kept it closed."

He meant Aspen Skiing Corporation, which controls the whole shebang. I was not about to weep for the losses of the Aspen Skiing Corporation.

We climbed in silence for a few minutes, and completed another circle over Big Burn. Skiers in their bright parkas stood out with supernatural clarity against the brilliant snow, looking about half an inch tall. Over on Powderhorn I could make out two ski patrolmen snowplowing their careful way down the hill with a canvas-covered aluminum toboggan between them. Someone else had got wiped out, but presumably not by a bullet.

These days, you never knew.

Pierce shifted in his seat and looked at me gravely. Here it came. "I suggested flying for a reason, Joe."

He's going to throw me out. "Oh?"

"It has been suggested to me that my place may be bugged."

If it was bugged, then they—the elusive they—knew about Blake's dying message.

"Who'd do a thing like that?"

"Whoever killed Blake. Whoever's trying to get you."

"Who do you guess that might be?" Play it dumb. He thinks you're dumb anyway. And maybe you are, accepting yet another invitation from someone you've been warned off of. "I'd just like to have ten minutes alone with 'em."

"I hope we'll both have that opportunity."

There was maybe a minute of quiet in the cockpit. We were heading southeast, toward Glenwood Springs, toward Denver. Then he changed the subject. "Did you know Sam Edwards well, Joe?"

"Not really. Martha and I were quite close when we were kids."

So close she got inside me deep enough you'd have to blast to get her out.

"She speaks very highly of you."

"It's mutual."

"There's a story—I never heard it from Sam, close as we were—but Martha mentioned it to me just yesterday. A time when she got thrown by a horse."

"Her palomino. I remember that. We were about fifteen. Her daddy made her get right back on."

"That's what she said. And in some funny way, Martha thinks that's why she ought to come back here. At least, that's what she says."

Pierce looked at me as though I might know some other, better reason why Martha might want to come back to Snowmass. He flattered me.

"Martha was never one to avoid unpleasantness."

"So like her daddy." He banked the plane again and made a dead set for Glenwood. "Martha," he went on, "just wanted to take this dirty old world in both little fists and give it a good scrubbing."

"You could say that."

"What a team they made, Blake and Martha! I have to say I didn't always agree with his politics, but hell, Joe Bird, I'm just an old conservative fogy. Still and all, there was something special about those two, a kind of a glow. You knew they had it in them to do great things."

So did Blake's killer, Austin. Was he you? "Somebody else thought they weren't so great, the things Blake planned."

"A terrible tragedy, Joe, a loss of national magnitude."

I could feel the pompousness rising in him like a pink tide, and the hypocrisy.

"I agree."

We were flying down the great picture-postcard alpine valley west of Snowmass past Mount Daly, gliding over ridges and valleys and snowfields and cliffs where it is completely possible no man has ever set foot, even in the old days when they'd dare anything looking for gold and silver in these defiant hills. There are truly wild places still in the Rocky Mountains, and that morning we flew over plenty of them. It would have been a fine place for killing: there was no one to see us but the wind.

Pierce moved the small aircraft through the updrafts and crosscurrents with the practiced ease of a trout gliding upsteam: the easier it looks, the more skill it takes. Like many things. I thought of the big golden eagle I'd seen over Ajax the day before, silent, a little threatening, working the wind for reasons of its own.

I would have given a lot to know just what Austin Pierce's reasons were for taking me up in his plane.

"She's very fond of you, Joe."

"We always did get on well."

"I think you may be able to help her in the days to come."

Fine. And who's going to help me? "Anything I can do, Mr. Pierce, I'll be pleased to."

"Call me Austin, please, Joe."

"Austin."

A game was being played, and I didn't even know how to keep score.

"She's really a good child. Of course, when you reach my advanced age, nearly everyone seems like a child."

"You look to be in pretty good shape to me." *Good enough to kill, maybe?*

"Well, we all do our best. I'm afraid my best isn't always good enough, though."

We were coming up on the Colorado River. I could see it gleaming blue in the distance, flecked with whitecaps and chunks of ice. Then it disappeared between the sheer rock walls of Glenwood Canyon. And suddenly it came to me that all the landscapes I'd loved in Aspen were discolored by the memory of sudden death. When would I ever be able to drive through that canyon again without sweating and flinching? Or ski Big Burn? Or turn the ignition key in a Porsche?

I looked at Pierce. He was looking straight ahead, the very

model of an alert pilot. *How many people do you know, Austin baby, named O'Leary?*

I started talking just to get my mind out of the clammy places it had been visiting. "Does Martha have any special plans?"

He kept looking straight ahead. "Permanent-type plans, you mean? I don't think so, Joe. It's a little soon for that. Martha says she needs quiet, a place to think it all out. That's why she wants to come here."

"To find peace?"

"God willing."

We had come right up on the Colorado River now, and Pierce banked the red plane in a half-circle to follow its cold blue progress. We lost some altitude, and he turned the plane as the river turned, idly, at random. The day was so clear you could see every rock and fir tree in perfect detail, and the ripples one by one, and their foam, the road and the railroad whose silver gleam rivaled the sunlight darting and glinting off the rushing water. I half-expected to see Vega's corpse waving from some rock.

My imagination hasn't had a whole lot of exercise all these years in Aspen. Most of my dreams and fantasies consist of wishing for even more perfect snow, or thinking up new combinations of ski trails on Ajax or Snowmass.

Now I found myself uncontrollably, compulsively inventing possible ways for people to kill me. People like Austin Pierce. I imagined the sudden appearance of a handgun, Pierce forcing me to jump out of the Cessna, of the stories he'd tell back in Aspen, of the people there who'd believe him, and who would not, his word against mine, and me dead. I imagined that what he'd said was true, about his place being bugged, only with him on the receiving end of the bugging, of his hearing my conversations with Martha, hearing Blake's dying warning, knowing I'd kept it to myself. I imagined Joe's place bugged: how else would they know we were going skiing yesterday morning and the coast would be clear to plant the bomb in my car? I thought these things, and the plane droned on, and Pierce kept silent, looking ahead the way a good pilot should, the faintest of smiles curling the edge of his lips.

The plane began climbing almost imperceptibly.

"It's a shame," I began, reaching in any direction to break

the silence, "that she hasn't any family: no kids, no brothers or sisters."

"She has me. We've always been just like kin."

"You've been very good for her, Austin." I managed to say it, but I didn't believe it. Austin Pierce must be pushing sixty. Maybe he'd pushed beyond it. But all of a sudden a nasty little thought bubbled to the surface of my newly fermenting imagination. *Suppose Pierce wanted Martha for himself?*

What better way than to make her a widow, than smother her with kindness, offering himself as the consolation prize?

Stranger things had happened, although I couldn't think of one right then and there.

It would be a motive.

I wondered, what no one seemed to know, precisely what were Austin Pierce's political connections? The surface was wealthy, Texan, and conservative. In other words, absolutely conventional. But maybe there was more to it than that. Maybe O'Leary had been so right that he'd been killed because of it. Maybe, since Blake Ross had come up like thunder as the Kennedy-type White Hope of the mid-1970's, someone decided to silence Blake forever before his influence peaked. And maybe that someone was named Pierce. I could never ask O'Leary, but I could, with luck, find out how O'Leary died. And the how might also be the why.

It seemed we'd been in Pierce's little plane for hours. The things unsaid between us crowded the cockpit: we were fencing without the honest clash of steel, without the possibility of drawing blood.

I still didn't know what he wanted from me.

It was nearly high noon. We were still following the canyon, but at a higher altitude. A train went west, a long freight, a perfect model train in a perfect model world. I imagined what Vega's corpse would look like by now, bouncing down the rapids, dragging over rocks, logged by water, honed on ice.

I was very tired of subtlety. "They've tried," I said, not looking at him but rather looking down, trying to find that special curve in the road where I'd become a murderer three nights ago, "three times now to kill me. Why do you suppose anyone would do a thing like that?"

He looked at me then. It was not a sympathetic look.

There was a pause, just a beat, but noticeable in the droning tension of the cockpit.

"The police," Pierce said quietly, "assume that whoever's behind all this thinks you're holding evidence that could upset their applecart, so to speak."

"If I were, you can bet the applecart would have been upset in about five minutes after they got Blake Ross."

"It's hard to convince guilty people of a thing like that, Joe. They don't operate on the same frequency as you and me."

Please God I never operate on the same frequency as Austin Pierce. "I guess not."

"Have you thought of taking a . . . little vacation?"

"It's been suggested. I wouldn't flatter them that much. And anyway, if it's the kind of setup I think it is, who's to say where I'd be safer?"

"What kind of setup is that, Joe? What you think is behind this?"

"I think it's a conspiracy, well-financed, whether private or political I couldn't say, and I think they're clever but not so clever as they'd like to believe, and I think they will trip themselves up fairly soon if they keep on after me, and I'll dance on their graves, if I am alive and able to dance."

"The police agree with you?"

"Some do. Some don't seem to have an opinion. My opinion, however, is well-recorded all over the place."

The plane began climbing again, and banked left 180 degrees and headed back toward Aspen. I couldn't tell whether I'd told Pierce what he came to find out, or whether he'd simply given up on me. More likely the latter.

"Well, now," he said, clucking like your maiden aunt, "and here I've been worrying about poor Martha when all the time you've been in grave danger. . . ."

"I've been lucky."

"Yes, I'd say you've been very lucky."

"Martha gets in this afternoon?" I knew the answer. I just wanted to change the subject: luck is a fragile thing, and if you talk about it too much, it tends to break.

"In about an hour. That's why we're going back."

"Anything I can do, Austin, I'll be glad to."

"Martha's a very fortunate girl to have a friend like you."

"And you." I'll never win a hypocrisy race, but nobody would ever be able to say I hadn't been in there trying.

"That's very kind of you, Joe."

Ten minutes later Pierce brought the red Cessna to a perfect landing on the Aspen airstrip. And ten minutes after that he dropped me at Joe's Place with a firm handshake, a confidential, man-to-man look in the eye, and these words: "I know I can count on you, Joe." Winston Churchill, sending the gallant troops into battle.

"Anytime."

"Thanks for your help, Joe, past and present. You'll be hearing from us."

Who was "us"? "Thanks for the ride." *Thanks for not killing me up there.*

"So long. Take care."

The big white station wagon sped back in the direction of the airport. Take care, indeed.

11

The door of Charlie's hospital room looked more forbidding than the Great Wall of China.

I stood outside it for a minute feeling faintly foolish, holding a big flowering plant, some kind of giant begonia, wondering what in the world to say. The doctor had been optimistic. There were no signs of brain damage, and even though the kid had lost nearly half of his right foot, the wound wouldn't be crippling. He'd be able to walk, even to ski. His shoes, his ski boots could be padded out to fit. It wouldn't be pretty, there would be pain sometimes, but when you considered what might have been the result of that bomb, things could have been very much worse.

He'd be in the hospital at least a month.

I knocked on the door.

"Come in." The voice was flat, sleepy. Drugged.

I came in. Charlie's bulk and his radiant energy had shrunk to something pale and flat under the blue hospital blanket and the pale sheets. He lay on his back, the right foot heavily bandaged and therefore bigger than the left, part of his hair shaved off to accommodate a bandage on his right forehead. There was another bandage on his right arm.

I was at my most eloquent. "Hi," I said.

"They missed." He said that and grinned, a ghost of Charlie's old grin maybe, but enough to warm the room. "You look," he went on, "like a fucking bridesmaid." I wonder what it cost him to say that.

I'd forgotten the flowers. I put the plant down on the windowsill. It was time for my touching speech. It's wonderful, being articulate. You can think of so many things not to say. "How are you feeling?"

"Nothing wrong with me a few beers and a girl wouldn't cure."

"I mean, really."

"I feel good, Joe. It's good to be alive. They've got me on something, shots of something, a drug, I don't feel pain, if that's what you're worried about."

That was only part of what I was worried about.

"I called your folks. They're out of town, in Japan."

"My folks have been out of town for a long, long time. Forever, as a matter of fact."

"Charlie, I'm sorry." He looked at me and the grin faded. It didn't have far to fade. "I know. Look, don't worry, okay? Charlie's gonna be fine. The doctor said that."

"You'll have to rest up a few weeks."

"I always was lazy. Joe?"

"What?"

"He wouldn't bullshit? The doctor."

"No. He said the same thing to me. You really will be okay. But it was close, very close. We were scared shitless. And they wouldn't let us be with you."

"I don't suppose there was a whole lot you could've done."

"Maybe not." Charlie's voice was drifting away. His eyes slid shut, then opened again. A nurse came in and said I'd have to be going now. I hated myself even more for the relief that came over me when she kicked me out.

"We'll be back later," I said, "Rita and Rick and me."

"Good." His voice was somewhere else. I turned to leave. "Joe?"

"I'm right here, kid."

"Take care of yourself, Joe."

"I'll do my best. And thanks."

"Thanks for the tree." He was drifting away again. The nurse touched my arm, convinced, beyond a doubt, that I was the carrier of unspecified but nevertheless sinister viruses.

"So long, Charlie."

Hank was still gone when I got back to Joe's Place in the jeep I'd rented. I made myself a sandwich and drank some coffee with it. The sandwich was good and so was the coffee and for all I noticed the tastes, I might have been eating sawdust. I thought of Charlie in that bed, of Pierce in his fancy little plane, of O'Leary dead, of Martha coming back, and what in the world my next move ought to be. Was a promise to Martha worth my life? It was something to think about.

The big old schoolhouse clock on the wall opposite the bar rang two o'clock. Two o'clock on Tuesday. I counted the days, nearly a week now since Blake and Martha came: Thursday, Friday, Saturday, Sunday, Monday, and today, Tuesday. The days made a little calendar of death and disruption. Two men dead for sure, Charlie almost, and no one in their right mind would be betting on my chances of making it to see another Thursday.

Rita came in with two big bags of groceries. I helped her unload, and told her about Charlie. We planned on visiting him in relays.

The phone rang. She picked it up, said hello, listened, frowned, hung up. "That," she said, "is very odd."

"Why odd?"

"They hung up. It's the second time that's happened."

"Some people are afraid to admit they've got the wrong number."

"If you say so."

"Paranoia," I replied, "is contagious."

"And I've got a bad case already, Joe. For one thing, I'm scared about Hank."

"Why Hank?"

"The old thing about, first you poison the watchdog before you do the burglary. He's been away since before you went for that plane ride."

"Hank can take care of himself." I would have said that about Joe Bird until last Thursday, but it didn't seem like the right time to share this charming thought with Rita.

"What did Pierce want?"

"It was a fishing expedition. I never quite learned what he wanted, and I'm not at all sure if he learned what he wanted from me."

"Sounds like tons of fun."

"Laugh a minute. He did say one thing: Martha's coming back here."

"You'd think," said Rita, "this would be the last place in the world she'd want to be."

"That's what I said."

"Unless there's some special reason."

I could feel her eyes on me as she said it, and I knew what she was getting at, and suddenly it dawned on me that I was like someone up to his chin in quicksand: struggling might only make me sink faster. What the hell: I struggled. I told her the story about falling off the palomino.

"Maybe that's it." There was enough doubt in her voice to fuel Ralph Nader for a year.

I sat quietly with a second cup of coffee while Rita moved efficiently around the bar and the kitchen. Then she came up behind my chair and put her hand on my shoulder. Instinctively I covered her hand with mine.

"What's up?" I asked.

"Come with me."

She took my hand and led me up the stairs as though I were a small boy caught raiding the cookie jar. She closed the bedroom door after us and sat me down on the edge of the bed.

"Shoes." She knelt in front of me and pulled them off.

"Socks." Off came my socks.

"Sweater." By now I was getting the message: it wasn't anything like my bath time.

She slipped out of her boots and blouse and blue jeans. The bright afternoon sun reached through the closed shutters of my bedroom and made tiger-stripe shadows over all the landscape of her body. It was a very inviting landscape.

Rita came close to me and put both long smooth arms around my neck and looked into my eyes.

"Life," she whispered, kissing me, "goes on." She was warm and very pretty, and I didn't need any encouraging. We lay in bold shadows with ease in the old knowledge that we fit together very well and with joy in the familiar surprises of a long wild journey that is always the same and forever new.

Then the phone rang.

On about the fifth ring I rolled over and picked it up.

"Joe?" It was Hank Wyland, and my relief at hearing his voice made me slower than I should have been to sense the fact that his voice was a new voice, sharply edged with concern. "I've got bad news, Joe. Listen. Mrs. Ross got in . . ."

My god. They'd gotten to Martha. "And what happened?"

"She wanted to go skiing right away. God knows why.

Anyway, she cracked up on top of Big Burn. It's pretty bad, Joe: she smashed into a tree. We're afraid to move her until a doctor gets up here."

"You were with her?"

"They got to me right away. Could you get up here quick? It might help. She keeps asking for you."

"Of course. Where are you?"

"Far left as you can go, heading up the hill. They call the trail Sheer Bliss."

"I'm on my way. Be there in less than an hour. . . . Hank?"

"Sure."

"Tell her I'm on my way, hear?"

"Done. I'll be waiting."

I was already out of the bed and reaching for ski clothes.

"What was that all about?" Rita sat up in bed.

"It was Hank. Martha's had an accident."

"I don't believe in accidents this week."

"You believe in Hank Wyland."

"Yeah." Her voice lacked conviction.

"Anyway, I'm going."

"Where?"

"Top of the Burn."

I pulled on socks, thermal underwear, ski pants, a wool turtleneck, and my old lucky red down parka.

"Joe? Don't go. Please?"

"I have to, honey, she's asking for me."

"Joe, I'm scared."

"You said that."

"I mean for you."

"I'll take care." She was standing now. I kissed her. "Do me a favor. Call Billy Medina and tell him where I went. Hank may not have the chance."

"Joe?"

"I've got to get moving."

"I love you."

She'd never said that before. I looked at her for an instant that seemed much longer than an instant.

"Thanks." Then I went clumping down the stairs. I looked back over my shoulder and saw her standing there at the top of the stairway, naked and lovely in the slanting shadows that fell through the shutters the way shadows must fall through jail bars.

If I hadn't gone down those stairs quickly, I might never have gone at all.

My rented Jeep bounced along the road to Snowmass like a stone skipped on water. I'd been in too much of a hurry to think when I turned on the Jeep's ignition, too busy to wonder whether some well-meaning friend had planted a bomb in this one. Maybe I was getting lucky, maybe they hadn't noticed me renting it.

I devoted every ounce of concentration on keeping the Jeep upright as I raced my fears through the darkening afternoon.

Rita loved me. Her words kept sneaking into my brain and being politely but firmly ejected again. That was a whole new ball game. That was something I couldn't deal with then, maybe not ever. That was breaking the rules of a game I'd invented, undermining the carefully constructed glistening icy igloo I'd built around what was left of my emotions.

Rita loved me. I decided not to think about Rita, and stepped on the gas.

I'll never learn.

It was a little after three when I got to Snowmass. I'd be lucky to make it to Big Burn before they shut the lifts down.

The bright clear morning had darkened. There was a new chill in the air and a pale gray haze. The sun was visible, but it looked like a flashlight seen through fog, receding. The wind was coming up, touched with the promise of a bitter-cold night. I wondered if they'd try bringing Martha down by chopper. That was done for the really bad cases. But it was done only in good weather: the crosswinds high up on the mountain made chopper-landing trickier than doing a Virginia reel in a live minefield.

People were looking at the sky with the kind of apprehension that made them decide not to take that last run. There was almost no line at number-two lift. My luck was holding.

I rode up number two with a little boy of maybe ten years who was bubbling over with his newfound enthusiasm for skiing. I asked his name.

"My name is Daring Derek."

"Okay, Daring Derek, tell me about the weather: is the sun going to come back out?"

He looked at me gravely, wide-set blue-gray eyes under a mop of dark brown hair, then decided to take me into his confidence. "I," he said solemnly, "have the sun in my pocket."

Maybe he did.

We talked about skiing the rest of the way up. At the top of number two, Daring Derek shot off the chair with the velocity of a missile, instructing me to have a good afternoon. Well, kid, I tried.

There wasn't much of a line at the next lift, either, but the quality of my liftmates was obviously taking a turn for the much worse. My shout of "Single!" conjured up a fifty-plus peroxide divorcée whose carefully preserved debutante giggle threatened to shatter my patience and my eardrums at the same time.

"I always say," she said, giggling, "that the nicest thing about ski places is, they're so democratic, I mean, one meets such fascinating types."

One sure does: killers, corpses, marked men. "That happens."

"I remember this absolutely darling instructor at Klosters—are you an instructor?"

"No."

"I thought, the red parka, the suntan, well, you look kind of like an instructor. What are you, actually?"

I'm a murderer, honey, and you may be next. "Actually, ma'am, I am an Indian."

"Ah! I should have guessed. India! How romantic. The Taj in the moonlight. The Ganges. Those naughty caves at—"

"Cherokee."

"Oh. That kind of Indian. Such a proud, tragic race. I always think there's something terribly . . . well, romantic about Indians, don't you think?"

"Terribly."

This monument to the cosmetics industry batted her three layers of eyelashes and chattered on. And somewhere up on the Burn Martha lay hurt, maybe dying.

I resisted the lady's invitation to a romantic glass of wine at the Sam's Knob restaurant and pushed off the chair with ungallant haste, confirming whatever dim prejudices she might have felt for the Cherokee nation. All the way around the first bend of the trail I was pursued by the sad mechanical merriment of her laughter.

They were just about to close off the lift line for the Big Burn chair when I scooted into it. There was less than a ten-minute wait. The late-afternoon air was cold at this altitude, and the wind was coming up ever sharper.

Daring Derek had been right about the sun: it was brighter now, but there was no warmth to it. I checked my watch: three-thirty on the button. It would be dark in an hour. There was no sound of choppers, no sight of the ski patrol or their toboggans. Maybe they'd gotten her down already. Maybe this was a goose chase, maybe she wasn't hurt so badly as Hank thought. Maybe.

I shared my chair with a talkative dentist from Salt Lake.

"Yessiree, must've been right about *here!*" He pointed into the woods with a hand trembling from vicarious thrills, with more ghoulish glee than accuracy, too soon by a football field's length for the place where Blake Ross met his bullet. I looked at the man and tried to suppress my anger. He was, after all, probably a perfectly decent law-abiding citizen. He'd probably never murdered anyone, which was more than I could say for myself. But there was something sickening in the delight he took in Blake's death. He was the kind of Sunday driver who slows to a crawl to gape at bad traffic accidents, smug in the sure knowledge that such messy misfortunes would never happen to him, God's favorite. "Yessiree, they say he up and died right in the chair. Could've been this very one we're in. Now, just think about that!"

"I'll do that."

"Terrible thing, that was."

"Terrible."

The chair seemed to be slowing down, or maybe it was nothing more than the short fuse of my patience speeding up in its race toward blind anger.

"Of course, there's some folks didn't exactly agree with the senator's political views, don't you know, he was a mite, well, let's call it progressive for some tastes, if you take my meaning. . . ."

"Was he?"

"Well, now, just havin' made your acquaintance, young feller, naturally I don't know your political views and all, begging your—"

"I don't have any political views." It was God's own truth.

"Well, now, isn't that something? No views!" He might have been speaking from the back of any campaign train making a whistle-stop tour of the Midwest about 1921. The chair murmured and clicked as it passed the tower that marked the place where they shot Blake. Every nerve in me contracted in unplanned anticipation of the next bullet, the one with my name on it. The dentist droned on, a curiously flat voice that somehow also managed to hold a note of whining: "Well, well, to each his own, young feller, said the old lady as she kissed the cow, ha-ha-ha!"

"Right."

I wondered about O'Leary, whether somewhere someone was activating an investigation of his death. I'd have Hank look into that today, and to hell with my promise to Martha.

"Dripped blood all up the ski trail, they say, although I wasn't here myself, Gertrude and me, that's Mrs. Grassner, well, Gert and me stopped over in Denver with her cousin Benjamin. Ben's very big in Denver. Got this electronics business, you know, only it's more than that. Why, I'll bet Ben's got a finger in just about . . ."

My tuning-out mechanisms proved to be in good working order.

The chair floated out over the big open snowfield that marks the midsection of Big Burn. No bullet. Yet.

The pale sun was moving lower and lower toward the jagged range of mountains to the west. A sharper wind caught us as we left the cover of the evergreen forest, swinging the chair, carrying the dentist's words out and over the valley, blessedly away from my ears, a ceaseless flow of words floating west toward an unsuspecting Salt Lake. In one way, dentists are like assassins: they do their best work on captive victims.

Rita loved me.

The wind scrubbed the big snowfields of the Burn, blowing and teasing the powder snow into dry little gusts, sending the fine white crystals streaming out horizontally from all the crests and moguls of the hill until it looked like the entire mountaintop was steaming and smoking and about to erupt.

The wind made the powder snow whirl and dance and take on a life of its own that had very little to do with gravity and very much to do with the violence of nature. The snow dervishes swirled around retreating skiers like white demon-escorts driving the last human invaders off the mountain. Well, almost the last. The icy crystals borne on icy wind reached up even to the slowly gliding chair. My face stung with the force of it. I turned away, covered my cheeks with my down-filled mittens.

The last of the day's skiers looked like ghosts themselves now, veiled in snow, half-hidden in the leaping puffs, driven by the searching wind. They might have been dancers gliding through a low, glittering fog made from bits of powdered crystal.

It was beautiful to see, cross-lit by the descending sun, but I knew what conditions like this were to ski in: cold and cruel, the wind-borne ice cutting your skin, the cold tugging at you, searching and pushing, icy-fingered pickpocket well-trained to steal all the warmth from your body.

I shivered and closed my eyes to the wind and wished for Martha Ross to be warm, wherever she was.

No helicopter was going to land on Big Burn in this weather.

Our chair swayed in the wind, and the wind hardly eased at all as we pulled into the second cut of woods on top of the Burn. It seemed even stronger, with more cutting edge.

People were skiing off the big open face of the Burn as fast as they could now. The wind punished lingerers.

I wondered where yesterday's eagle kept himself on afternoons like this.

Our chair pulled up to the unloading ramp, and I skied off to the left with never a good-bye to the Salt Lake dentist.

I started on a trail called Timberline, cutting as far toward the edge of the area as I could, heading where Hank told me to head, toward the boundary-line trail they'd named Sheer Bliss. I skied across the top face of the mountain, carefully, not too fast for fear of missing Hank, wondering if they'd taken Martha down on the toboggan after all, and, if they had, would Hank have left a message or a messenger for me?

I kept on my straight, nearly horizontal path across the trails, nearly at right angles to the fall line, just descending enough to give me momentum, skiing easy and nearly upright, working the hill by just letting my skis edge slightly into one long, smooth, controlled sideslip on their slippery scientific-wonder bottoms, moving across the face of the mountain with an uncanny gliding motion despite the wind, moving like something on tracks, a duck in a shooting gallery, a very easy target, if anyone needed practice.

But that wasn't what they had in mind.

I kept gliding until the motion took me under the secondary Burn chairlift, number-nine, and on the far edge of Sheer Bliss. There was an orange sign: "DANGER. AREA BOUNDARY. DO NOT SKI BEYOND THIS POINT. ASPEN SKIING CORPORATION." No Hank. No Martha. No ski patrol. I waited, looking first uphill, into the wind, then downhill, then across the Burn in the direction from which I'd come. Nothing.

The far edge of Sheer Bliss is a wall of tall spruce backing onto a big ridge.

The wind hissed and wailed through the evergreens. I could hardly see another skier. It was just past four o'clock. Soon the patrol would scrub the mountain. I wondered how long Hank expected me to wait. I decided fifteen minutes would be fair. Then I did a little warm-up routine, knee bends, a few long forward stretches, a couple of hops-in-place.

The temperature when I'd left Joe's Place was under twenty degrees. This much later, this much higher, it had to be hovering near zero. Not to mention wind chill. You could get frostbite just standing up on a day like that.

Maybe five of my scheduled fifteen minutes had passed, very slowly, when a tall, lean, and beautifully familiar shape emerged from the blowing powder up the trail and glided toward me in company with the sad music of the wailing wind.

Hank Wyland didn't even say hello, just skidded to a halt and waved me on. "This way, Joe."

It was a command, but Hank's job was giving commands. I followed quickly, glad for some action, any action.

Hank skied on ahead, skiing easy, not pushing it, moving

fluently in and out of the dense evergreen clusters that grace the far side of the trail, heading downhill maybe two hundred yards from where he'd found me, cutting into deeper woods. I couldn't see the Sheer Bliss trail at all now. I wondered how they'd ever found Martha in this forest.

The clumps of trees got thicker and less picturesque, but at least they cut the wind a little. The wailing wind muted to a whining, and the ice crystals didn't cut quite so hard.

Suddenly Hank turned right, cut between two huge spruce trees into a small clearing marked at its far edge by a big gray, jagged, weathered stump. A lightning-struck spruce. Hank pulled up just beyond that stump, into a little hollow more or less sheltered from the wind, and very definitely sheltered from casual observation, if there were any skiers left on Snowmass to observe.

I spoke first. "Where is she, Hank?"

"Be still, Mr. Bird."

The voice that replied wasn't Hank's voice, but familiar all the same. Too familiar. It was Gart's voice, the boss of the flunky I'd run into the river. Gart's voice came from right behind me, from behind the stump, and the hard round thing pressing into the base of my spine was no banana.

I looked at Hank Wyland. "What the hell is this?"

"I'm real sorry, Joe." Hank turned to look at me better, and something flickered across his cool, honest, wide-set eyes, some emotion, maybe pity. "It wasn't anything we planned, Joe. Shucks, you just happened to be in the wrong place at the wrong time."

"So you shoot me for that?"

"I don't think we'll shoot you, Joe. Not unless you leave us no other choice. There's been enough shooting. You're going to have a little accident, that's all."

A little accident. In zero weather on an empty Snowmass. Hank had a gun on me too, a regulation police revolver. My bodyguard. Good old trusty Hank. I would have followed him anywhere, and had. He must have counted on that.

Gart spoke, his soft ominous whisper. He was liking this. It was his kind of show. "Move ahead, Mr. Bird, and to your left, and very, very slowly. It would be most unwise to try anything."

It might be more unwise not to try something.

They'd picked their spot well. With two guns on me, there was no way to ski fast enough or erratically enough through the tight groves of trees to dodge their bullets. On an open slope I might have tried it.

Whatever Gart was jabbing in my spine stayed there as we moved around that stump. For a moment there was silence. All we could hear was the whispering wind.

Then came a more familiar sound, the cries of the ski patrol as they made their final sweep of the mountain, clearing every trail to be sure no injured strays were left to spend the night on the windstruck mile-high slopes of Snowmass.

You could freeze to death on Snowmass on a night like tonight was going to be. Someone was betting pretty heavily on that.

One patrolman must have come within twenty-five yards of us, yodeling happily at the end of his long day. My day looked like it was ending too, all my days, all my nights, and the ski-patrol guy might have been a thousand miles away, for all the good he did me.

The next voice I heard was Hank's. "A little farther."

The gun pressed more urgently into my back, and we moved through the trees to a place that was a little more open, a place with a few ski tracks, and a steeper slope. I looked at Hank, figuring my chances of making a break for it and succeeding. They were not good. Hank was looking past me, over my shoulder somewhere. The pressure on my spine lessened, vanished altogether. Hank nodded in the direction of what I thought was empty space over my left shoulder. I was wrong.

The space wasn't empty at all. It was filled with something very hard and very fast that swung noiselessly through the air and struck me a tremendous wallop on the back of my head, at the base of my skull, on the left.

Lights flashed, music played, and I had a lovely warm feeling as I floated and drifted in long lazy spirals down a bottomless hole. I found myself wondering, almost idly, what Martha might be doing right then.

My skull has always been thicker than most people's. If it hadn't been, maybe I wouldn't have been quite so eager to march into every damnfool trap these thugs set up for me. I was dazed and very shaken, but not quite out. The cool cushion of new snow revived me a little. But some instinct told me to lie still as death. Something warm was trickling down my neck. Something cold was crawling up my spine: plain old hundred-proof fear.

My performance as an unconscious ski bum must have been convincing. They began talking as if I were already dead.

"Mr. Olympic Skier seems to have had an accident," Gart explained in his low, sexless voice. "Very dangerous, skiing alone. Seems like he smashed into this tree. Lost a ski. Broke a leg. Which one, Mr. Wyland?"

So Hank was Mr. Wyland, just as I was Mr. Bird. I wondered where he fit in this very weird scheme of things, who outranked whom. Gart seemed to be asking Hank, not telling him.

Hank's reply wasn't long in coming. This was obviously a subject he'd given some thought to. "His right leg's all fucked up anyway. Get the left one."

Hank's voice was casual, contemptuous. My buddy. Someone grabbed me by the collar and dragged me a few feet until my head was resting against the icy trunk of a big evergreen. My possum performance continued. Someone fumbled with my left ski binding.

"Mr. Bird just lost a ski."

"That was pretty careless of him." Hank's voice had lost a lot of its country-boy simplicity. It had turned into something cold and scary. I began plotting my next move, as much as you can plot with your head half-broken and one ski gone.

I heard a sort of swishing noise that must have been my left ski starting a long, lonesome journey down the mountain. I would have given everything I owned, and plenty that I didn't own, to be on it.

"Now do his leg." Hank's voice had a kind of quiet triumph in it. I shouldn't have outskied him yesterday. "And," Hank continued, "do it right, Gart. Like a real accident. Below the knee. If you fuck up like you did with Ross, we're all in trouble."

"I can't help it if someone beat me to him. For Chrissakes, at least he's dead."

"Not as Mr. Pierce arranged it, Gart, not neatly. Messily.

With too many loose ends dangling. Like the gentleman at your feet. Now, do it."

"Is one leg going to be enough?"

"Will you do it, or shall I?"

I didn't hear whatever it was he used as a club. There was a sharp cracking sound, a double-barreled crack that was first the sound of wood hitting bone, and then the sound of bone breaking.

A great shudder went through me.

This time I didn't have to fake going under. A wave of pain rushed through me, quickly followed by numbness. I felt dizzy all over again, went under and came up a little, then went under deeper and deeper, struggled to come out of it, then lost whatever small grip I'd had on consciousness, maybe on life itself.

Hank's voice was the last thing I remember, giving Gart his final instructions: "Throw a little snow on him. Better they don't find him for a few days. Or a few months. They say it'll go down to twenty below tonight." Good old Hank. He might have been telling someone how to decorate a cake.

The pain was less now, and therefore more scary. It was turning into shock, and the shock plus the cold would very likely do what Hank hoped it would. Every deep got a little deeper, the ups got shallower and shorter, until finally I didn't feel anything at all.

12

Martha's voice floated up to me faintly through long tunnels. But something had chilled the warmth in her voice and darkened the color of it.

"Why, it's Joe. Joe Bird!" Martha walked into Joe's Place with Blake. Martha greeted me.

"I want you on my team, Bird. You'll start in the downhill next Saturday."

That was another voice from another time, the voice of a coach at Boulder.

"Joe. Be careful." Rita's voice, a little choked-up.

"Do you know what I mean to do when I grow up, Joe Bird? I am going out into the world and change it." Martha's voice, a long-ago Martha.

My mind, it slowly dawned on me, must be breaking up and shaking out all the little fragments of memories I'd stored there without realizing it, all these years. A dog barked, a familiar bark. I would have known that barking anywhere. Goliath, my old yellow Labrador, dead these twenty years. Golaith, to whom everything was a pleasant surprise, Goliath chasing his tail around and around in my mother's kitchen in Eagle Grove, when he and I were youngsters and the world was filled with promises.

The cold darkness in my head began forming into images. Eight tall gray grain elevators got themselves painted pink every night by the long slow prairie sunset, but they still all said "EDWARDS" eight times in huge blue letters.

"I love you." Rita. Again. I mustn't forget that. That was useful information. I looked from Rita into the nearest of the grain elevators. It was filled with ten-dollar bills.

"It's hard to convince guilty people of a thing like that, Joe," said the smoothly educated voice of Austin Pierce.

"They don't operate on the same frequency as you and me." Right on, Austin baby.

"Life," said Rita, kissing me, "goes on." Pray for it, Rita.

"Naturally, his politics were a mite . . . well, progressive for some folks . . ." the dentist from Salt Lake droned on over the racing wind.

Something churned in whatever was left of my head. I began wondering if I was dead, if these voices were simply keeping me busy on the express trip to hell.

"So romantic, don't you think? Moonlight on the Taj . . ." A lady on the make on the ski lift.

"I," said Daring Derek confidentially, "have the sun in my pocket."

I wondered if I'd ever see another sunrise. At least the voices were getting more recent. Maybe that meant something. So far, all the activity was in my head. It was time to try something physical. If I was ever going to get off this mountain, I'd have to move my ass somehow. I started with something easy. I tried to move my head.

My cheek seemed to be stuck to the tree trunk. Frozen. I waited, gathering up a few scraps of courage. It was going to hurt.

I suddenly jerked my head to the right. Skin tore. At first there was no pain at all. Then a burning. Warm blood on my cheek. The only warm thing on me, maybe the only warm thing on Snowmass Mountain. And draining away. There had been blood enough on this mountain. I had a feeling there was going to be more blood spilled, and with luck, not all of it mine.

The next engineering project was getting my eyes open. Couldn't do it. Snow and frozen tears iced them shut. Tried to move my arm. Right arm. Wiggle fingers. Left arm. Same drill. Fingers wiggle-able. Barely. Good: they aren't frozen solid, that's one thing. One small thing.

Slowly, slowly, my right arm made the long climb up to my face. The down mittens still on. My mouth, at least, opens and shuts. The mitten makes it to my mouth. Hold it in my mouth. Off with the mitten. Warm hand rubs my eyes, rubs the ice to melting. Now my face is wet, melted snow, blood from my torn cheek. Now my eyes open.

There is nothing to see.

Blackness. I can hear. I can hear my breath. Working too hard, just lying there like a toad in winter. Well, hell, it is winter. At least toads have the use of their legs. I see a dingy kind of gray that has to be snow. And nothing but blackness beyond that. I try to remember directions. I'm lying facing down the mountain, more or less. Meaning the trail boundary is on my right. Meaning it's a long crawl back to the Big Burn lift, which would be the most direct way down the mountain. If I'm that lucky. If crawling isn't beyond me. There is a faint whining sound, a lost-soul-in-torment sound.

I turn my head to the right, turn it up a little.

Trees. Great tall pointy spruces, black against a blue-purple sky. The trees are moving. The whining noise is the wind, restless, the searching wind moving through the trees like it's looking for a lost lover. Certainly not looking for me. Would anyone be looking for me? Why hadn't Rita blown the whistle? She knows where I am. Where I went, anyway.

Forget Rita. Move your damn legs. Can't feel my left leg at all. Rubbed snow on my cheeks. Hand moves back into the mitten. Some warmth there, maybe a little more, it's hard to tell. Wiggle toes. Now I hear Hank's voice, good old Hank, old buddy, chum, pal: "His right leg's all fucked up anyway. Do the left one."

But I can feel my right toes, Hank. It isn't that fucked up. They actually move. But nothing on the left. All gone. Maybe frozen. Nothing at all, not even pain. Pain would be welcome, it'd mean something's alive down there. Thanks a lot, Hank.

Right ski still on.

Poles? Grope for 'em. Pole number one all present and accounted for, sir. Pole number two absent without leave, sir. Where did that come from? Wasn't even in the Army. Maybe I should have been. Grope. Hope. There it is. Pole number two reporting, sir. You betcha. Wiggle. Flex. Maybe. Just maybe.

The left leg has to be splinted. How?

Wristwatch. It is seven-fifteen. The sky is less black than before; or before, maybe the blackness was in my head. Black thoughts.

I see a star. The sky, then, is clearing up. Maybe there'll be a moon. Moon. Soon. Wow, poetry. Three-quarter moon?

Can't remember last night. Why should I? Last night was a million years ago. Last night I was alive. Tonight I'm not sure.

Someone thinks I am not. Alive.

And where the heli's the moon? Or is the moon in on the plot too? Might as well be. Join the team.

I lay there against the tree trunk flexing and wiggling every part of me that could still flex and wiggle.

My mind came back faster than my body, became a kind of half-frozen computer, scanning, scanning, riffing through a hundred schemes to get me off that big empty mountain. Or anyway, living through the night.

I knew where I was, and the knowledge scared me. As far away from any kind of help as you could be on Snowmass. I'd skied every inch of the mountain, knew it the way you know a lover's body. Knew its pleasures, its surprises, its dangers. Knew them too well. The hill was generously sprinkled with ski-patrol emergency telephones, clearly marked, on trees, on poles, on some of the stanchions that held up the chair lift. But who was going to man a ski-patrol phone when the mountain was three hours closed tighter than a drum? But maybe they did keep the damn thing manned. They might be that careful. I simply didn't know. It was a chance. And I couldn't pass up any chance, however slight.

Damned if I could remember where the nearest patrol phone was. How many times had I skied carelessly past those well-marked phones? One, I knew, was right in the middle of the Burn, next to a small clump of spruces. At about this height. And another, maybe more likely, on one of the stanchions of the Big Burn lift. And at the base of the lift, for sure. That would make the most sense. If I could get myself going. Crawling?

I didn't have any idea whether I could even stand up, let alone move.

Slowly, slowly, inching my fucked-up right leg in under me to get the full weight, leaning against the tree trunk, gathering both poles in my right hand for more leverage, I half-pushed, half-pulled, half-willed myself upright.

Try it some black frozen night on a windswept eleven-thousand-foot-plus mountain with one leg smashed and the other aching like to kill.

Success. A few more successes like that and I'd be a screaming maniac just from pain. If not despair. If not rage.

Rita loves me. If she loves me so much, where the hell is she?

Still couldn't feel the left leg. Can't use the ski poles for a splint. On one ski, I'm going to need both poles. For sure. A branch, maybe I can break one off. To be tied with what? No belt. The parka has drawstrings. Lucky old old-fashioned parka. Lucky red parka. Hood drawstrings, waist drawstrings, bottom drawstrings. Lucky red parka. "Are you a ski instructor?" No, lady, I'm a murderer. Or murder victim. A semi-murder-victim. Three-quarters done, at the most conservative estimate.

The sky is getting lighter. I can make out individual trees. There are more stars now. The moon must be getting higher. Not far from me, on top of the snow where it has no reason to be, is a long, thick dead branch. Maybe too long. Maybe too heavy. But a branch, and here, close enough.

I shuffle and slide, dragging the broken left leg, poling with both poles, struggling to keep my one ski at right angles to the slope of the mountain. Hate to leave the support of the tree trunk. Pole, drag, slide, inch by precious inch. Keep that ski edged, dummy. You want to break a leg or something? Made it to the old branch. Now comes my well-known one-leg knee bend as I grope to pick it up.

Heavier than I'd thought. But reasonably straight. They're just not making splints like they used to. Got the damn thing up, dragged it and myself to another tree trunk, leaned on it, sighed, cursed, groaned a little, no point in gallantry, no one here to hear, pulled the drawstrings out and with them some of the warming capacity of my good old lucky red parka, because now it would be flapping open, not that that really mattered, I'd be moving, working up a sweat. Hopefully.

Around and around. Damned shame I wasn't ever a boy scout. Knots. Am I cutting off circulation? How can you tell when you can't feel the damn thing anyway? Does it matter? If it's frozen, the leg, maybe it's a loss already. Charlie and me, with two good legs between us. Save a fortune on skis. Done. Drawn and quartered. Anyway, it's lashed to the mast, splinted, it won't be flapping in the wind like the banner of a defeated regiment. Bravo, Bird. Full speed ahead. Maybe your leg will freeze itself back together, just think of that.

No. On second thought, don't think of that.

Don't think about anything except getting off this hill.

Now.

I pushed off from my resting place, resolutely blocking out all the facts I knew by heart, by instinct, of just how far I had to go.

If I'd thought about it seriously, I might never have pushed off at all.

Poling, sliding, not skiing, really, a kind of shuffle, dragging the splinted leg slowly, slowly, always trying hard to keep a horizontal plane, right angles to the slope, knowing the worst danger would be moving fast, moving down.

And there were about three thousand vertical feet to move down. Somehow.

How many times had I cleverly worked out the longest possible runs down Snowmass? I could play the hill like a flute, until the trails spun out into mile after mile of powdered magic.

Thinking up shortcuts wasn't my game. Until now, until this bloody night. I'd have to cut under the number-nine lift to the Burn lift and try to get down it, or one of the trails next to it. Which would lead me by a relatively direct route down the trail named Monkshood into the Banzai cutoff to the West Village of Snowmass. To the Pierce house. To *what?*

It felt good to be moving, hope grafted on top of the pain and the rage.

Pole, pull, drag, slide. Like some kind of perverted dance step. The Crippled Crawl. I knew, somewhere at the bottom of the well where my fears lived, that my aptly described fucked-up right leg would never hold up for the entire crawl down Snowmass. I also knew I didn't know what else to do. So I moved slowly, trying very hard not to think what would happen when the leg failed.

Pole, pull, drag, slide.

My eyes were getting to feel more at home in the darkness. I could feel the hill. I could see the trees and, not far ahead, the shape of one tower of lift nine. Which left about three football fields to the Big Burn lift. I was out of the trees now.

Open snow, packed snow, skied-on snow. At least if I crumped out here, someone would find me.

It wouldn't make world headlines, but it was progress.

A trail. Trails made for skiing, gliding, soaring. And here comes old Joe Bird, crawling. The temptation was seductive. To ski! You can ski on one ski. Amputees do it all the time. And maybe I'd soon be one, so the practice might help. Don't be more stupid than usual, Bird. Do not aim yourself down this trail. I risked a small glide, a level little glide, still horizontal, but a glide nevertheless. Wow. Huge, record-setting distances were vanishing under my ski. Two, three feet at a time! The shuffle became a kind of a lope. Still poling, still pulling, but now I was gliding, sliding longer distances across the packed snow. Moving, maybe, at a slow walk. But compared to what I had been doing, it was flying.

It was also using up more energy than I could afford. I knew that, knew it was unwise, knew it was getting to be a race between making more progress now and getting more tired, sooner.

But I kept on gliding. Because it had always been that kind of race.

The moon came up and cheered me.

It rose quite suddenly from behind the next mountain, and my gray blurred mountaintop world got much brighter, crisper, bolder. The snow gleamed white now. The big trees actually cast shadows. It was a bright three-quarter moon and it was smiling on me.

I paused for a minute, breathing hard. The moon threw magical purple shadows from the huge black spruce trees. Moonlight and starlight, and all Aspen down below. Beautiful. Think of all the ugly places people die in, Joe. No. Don't think. Move out.

I moved out. More steadily now, the rhythm came easier now, if you could call such a jerky motion rhythmic. Whatever it was, it was a kind of progress. It was taking me closer to help, to revenge, to—what?

I was past the number-nine lift now, still cutting across the face of Big Burn toward the Burn lift. Which had to be there, not terribly far away, even though I couldn't see it. Pole, pull, glide, drag. But anyway, moving.

And there was the Burn lift. Something gleamed up ahead,

a hard metallic gleaming, the pylon for the chair lift, chairs hanging empty from their ice-sheathed cable, one chair with Blake Ross's blood on it. A row of empty chairs, all that was left of a party from which the guests had long since gone home, or to heaven, or hell, ghost chairs hanging empty in the cold glare of moonlight.

I could hear Blake's dying words: "O'Leary was right . . ."

And where the hell was O'Leary this night? I thought of the haunted mad woman's voice on the phone: "He has a new address in Arlington now, hee-hee . . ."

This was not a cheering thought.

Pole, pull, drag, glide.

What, exactly, was O'Leary right about? So right that someone had killed him because of it?

I wondered how to start up a chair lift. From the bottom. First you'd have to get to the bottom. Down the lift line. Kamikaze. I remembered last Thursday morning, before Blake, before the world blew to hell, skiing this lift line, the speed of it, the swift grace, the gliding arrogance, showing the tourists how it's done. It was done, all right.

There must be a way, a better-than-dragging way. A way down the lift line. To the patrol phone I knew was at the bottom. To the shortest distance between two points, between despairing and hoping, maybe between death and life. It's an emergency, Officer, a matter of life or death.

I was getting dizzy again. The big painted steel pylon blurred in front of me. Pole, pull, drag, glide. Now I was touching it, leaning on it, feeling the blessing of rest. How good it feels, not straining; how much better it would feel, lying down. Just for a minute. Closing eyes.

And never waking up.

Maybe there was a faster way down. Sitting. Gliding on the one ski, using it like a toboggan. The hot-dog skiers, the ski-ballet freaks did something like that, crouching, sitting back on their skis. It was possible.

I sat on the right ski, the only ski, carefully positioning the splinted left leg in front of me. Knowing that one good jolt might break the good leg, or destroy the broken one, if it wasn't destroyed already. There was still no feeling in that left leg, not even pain.

Take it easy. Very easy. Poles clutched tight about a foot

up from their baskets. Pull, drag the poles, brake with the poles, don't, for God's sake, get going too fast. Watch it! That's better. Tower to tower, no sign of the patrol phone. How many towers? Ten? Thirty? A million? Three towers. Now four. Enjoy yourself, Joe Bird, this could be your last ski trip.

The lift line cut a white streak through the blackness of the same spruce forest that had served Blake's killer so well. And Blake's killer hadn't been Gart, after all. Then who? Someone got to him first, said Gart. Why wouldn't he take the credit all the same? Two conspiracies, both after Blake Ross? Why two? Why any? Why was Blake worth killing, and at such risk, such expense of planning, such involvement of people, such killing off of innocent bystanders? Five, six, seven poles crept by. I was making progress by feet now instead of inches, but they were slow feet, straining feet.

Now I could see the bottom. Three poles down. The clearing. The little hut that held the lift machinery and, I was sure, a phone.

At the last tower before the lift hut at the bottom I decided to stand up and risk skiing. The joy of overconfidence. Snow too deep, crusted, unskied-on here, even by healthy people with two good legs and two good skis. Started too fast. The heavy splint screwed up whatever was left of my balance. Smash. Great big header facedown onto the crust, which is to say ice. Down and out. Blacked out. Out-out. Don't know how long. Be a long time before I try one of those again, like never. If I live to see never.

Up again. Barely. The snow was nearly level now. Pole. Pull, drag, drag. No gliding. Inch by agonizing inch I made it toward the little hut, a hard dark shape against the moonlit sky.

There had to be a phone in there.

The lift hut was small, dark, empty. And locked. I broke the window in the door and let myself in.

Only when I tried to step inside did I realize my right ski was still on. I looked at it in wonderment, a Martian discovering skis for the first time. Then I bent, using the ski pole for a cane, and released the binding. Undid the safety strap. Wondered if I'd ever put skis on again.

Stepped into the hut. There was the patrol phone, on the wall, waiting.

It was alive, hooked up, buzzing with electricity, throbbing with hope. The only live thing on this forsaken hill but for me, and I wasn't making too many bets on me. Pick up the phone. Wait. Buzz-buzz, crackle-crackle.

"Hello? Hello! Anyone there? Anyone." Nothing. Zero. Zip. Hell, why should they man the damn phone all night long? Who but a maniac would be up on Snowmass at night? Who, indeed?

I stood in the dark hut for a moment, listening idly to the electric crackle of the phone. Then I felt something warm on my cheek. Tears. I thought of staying in the hut, but it was a short-lived idea. I'd freeze to death just as surely in there as I would outside.

Slowly, numbly, moved out of the hut. Forced my head to turn, forced my eyes into focus. Wiped off the last stupid tears. At least they were warm. At least they indicated there was something alive and churning inside me.

It was a little warmer there, down off the peak, below the tree line. Or maybe it was the rage burning in me, generating another kind of heat. Okay, crybaby. You've made some progress. Hell, you're nearly halfway down the damn hill.

Only it isn't a hill. It is a very big mountain, inhabited by killers. And you've used up more than half of your energy.

Then I saw it.

Over there. By the loading platform. That shape. Leaning. Funny-looking. Move, dummy. The canvas cover. Of? Wow. Thank you, someone, whoever, God. Thank you very much.

It was an aluminum ski-patrol toboggan.

The patrol stashes extra toboggans at the top and the bottom of every lift. I knew that, or should have known, but hadn't remembered. A toboggan! Long and light and strong as rocks. And waiting. Designed by experts to evacuate the wounded. Well, Joe Bird, you qualify. Eminently. It wouldn't be easy. But it had to be a lot easier than what I had been doing.

I untied the canvas, tore off the tarp, flipped over the toboggan, and just about flipped myself in the process. It was bigger than I'd thought, with a gondola curve to the bow and sides that curved generously to support the passenger. The curving sides would be a problem when the passenger was also the sole means of locomotion. The toboggan was designed, and designed well, to be pulled by a patrolman skiing in front of it, and restrained by another patrolman in the rear. I'd have to lie flat on my gut with right leg pushing and my right arm poling, and try to steer the damn thing at an angle.

Still, it would be better than the dragging, crawling, inch-by-inch routine I'd been doing.

I took my ski and the extra pole and stowed them in the far side of the toboggan. The splinted leg took some thinking. Whatever damage Gart had done to it, and whatever worse things I'd done, dragging it halfway across Snowmass in a make-do splint, I didn't want to make it worse.

Finally I lowered myself to a sitting position, slowly, with the help of the ski pole, facing the rear end of the toboggan. Down and down, inch by inch. Then I swung the right leg into the shell of the toboggan and pulled the splinted left leg in after it. I lay back and slowly rolled over. Good. The left leg was giving me some pain. Maybe it was coming back to life at last.

Now I was in the right position: facing the front, right leg overboard, right arm clutching its ski pole, the left leg resting as comfortably as it could on the padded bottom. Steering would be worse than awkward: the broken leg didn't allow for much shifting of weight. I'd have to lurch a lot. Well, lurching was getting to seem natural to me.

I pushed off, pushed hard, thinking of all the other times I'd ridden downhill on some poor ski patrol's toboggan: four fractures, any number of pulled ligaments, one broken collarbone, and Grenbole. I'd fucked up then, too.

The base of the Big Burn lift is nearly level, and the runoff trail that leads down the mountain, Monkshood, is easy, a commuter run that curves down around the bottom of the chair lift, down and down in a gentle series of cascades, the kind of run even intermediates don't give a second thought to. I'd skied that trail so many hundreds of times without giving it any thought at all that I couldn't for the life of me remember exactly how it wound its way down the mountain.

I had plenty of opportunity to find out.

Now every mogul was a challenge. Every curve and rise

and sudden dropoff became a major event, a new threat to be faced and calculated and attacked with the cunning and bravado of some rebel bandit attacking a very well-fortified bunker. Taking a bump or a dip or a curve right could mean the difference between making it and spilling, between getting down the mountain and things I'd rather not think about even now. Knowing this did not make it easier.

The toboggan crunched and grated over the icy crust. Hank Wyland had been right about his twenty below. It felt like a million below.

The toboggan slid fast and easy once it got going. Sometimes too fast, too easy. Too hungry for the bottom. I damn near pulled my right leg out of its socket, desperately braking with my foot. The toboggan wanted the bottom of the mountain, sought it like some homing missile. I wanted the bottom too. Only, I had a vested interest in being alive when I got there.

The prow or whatever it is you call the front of a toboggan curved up so steeply I couldn't see over it unless I leaned far out to the right side.

I lurched and skidded down the first cascade of the trail, and if anyone had been watching, it would have looked like a pretty drunken performance. And in a way I was drunk, drunk with anger and fear and some blind gut-deep fever just to keep on living a few minutes longer.

It had all come down to that, minutes, seconds. I'd stopped counting time in hours or days or weeks. The bottom of Snowmass was the only fixed thought in my head. I had no plans, or even hopes about what I'd do when I got there.

If I got there.

The toboggan snaked its way down the first big drop in the trail, a fall of moguls that gave onto another kind of runoff, fairly flat, requiring more pushing, tougher legwork, until the trail began to slope a little more steeply. The toboggan picked up some speed, but good speed this time, not reckless speed. Or maybe I was finally learning how to handle the big awkward tin boat. We were running on the side of the toboggan instead of on its bottom, leaning heavily to the right, and that slowed us down, made the steering tougher. But we were moving three or four times faster than I ever could have moved alone. It was working. I was getting there. Maybe only God and the cold moon knew where I was getting, or what I was getting into, but somehow that didn't seem to matter. Especially not to the good old toboggan.

The toboggan moved relentlessly on, traversing a big slow curve that wrapped itself around the fat waist of Snowmass Mountain. Far below, from behind a distant rise, came a glow that had to be the lights of the West Village.

For the first time that night it began to sink into my thick skull that maybe it wasn't time for me to die just yet.

I was more than halfway down the mountain now, maybe two-thirds of the way down. The worst part was behind me.

I've never bothered to measure the trail I was sliding down now, the bottom of Monkshood and into the Banzai cutoff. However long it is, I made it longer by crossing and recrossing every slope that looked anything like steep, hating every extra inch this necessary traversing added to the long downhill run, but growing more cautious now that I could feel my goal coming almost within sight.

I felt alive now, alive and burning up with hate.

From time to time I'd pause, even though the toboggan wanted to go on down, crunching eagerly as though it were eating the very snow we rode on. I'd pause and get my breath back a little and let my agonized right leg rest a little. The moon was full up now, still bright, still smiling.

Then I'd push on carefully. Something inside me was flashing quick hot warnings: *don't blow it now.* I had a feeling that if I crashed again, blacked out again, got off the track again, it would almost surely be for good.

I wasn't going to give Hank Wyland that satisfaction. Push, crunch, coast, drag the foot, lurch, push off again, coast some more, drag foot, push. I had the rhythm of it now. I'll never claim it was fun, that toboggan ride, but at least by now it was easier. I allowed myself to hope a little.

I thought of Rita.

The toboggan lumbered down a slope and up a rise. Now I could see the lights from the village. Now there were three choices of runoff trails to take. They all led to the village.

The one on the right would lead to the Pierce house.

The wind was dying down, and moonlight poured sharp and clear over glittering crusts of snow. I got tired of pretending to think rationally and simply let instinct take over. Instinct and rage.

Logic might have said: *go for the village, go for a cop.*

Hank Wyland was a cop. So much for cops.

I took the trail on the right.

I pushed with my throbbing right leg, and the toboggan slid through a wide splash of moonlight into the picket-fence shadows of an aspen grove, then back to the other side of the gently sloping trail again, back and back, crisscrossing the not-very-wide ski trail for the length of maybe four football fields, then slamming rather fast around one final curve and lumbering up the far-left-hand banked side of the trail, moving like some demented tortoise, lurching finally to rest in a pool of deep shadows some fifty yards up the slope and across the trail from the huge picture windows of Austin Pierce's house.

For a moment I just lay there, with my head down, safe in shadows, clutching the edges of the toboggan like the safety device it was, blanking out all thoughts, wondering, because this was surely my last chance to wonder, if it still wasn't a better idea to go straight down to the village.

But clamping my eyes shut didn't make the Pierce house go away, or the evil in it. And biting my lip did nothing to quell the silent screams inside me.

I raised my head.

I opened my eyes.

I was on a rise just slightly up the hill and across the trail from the main living-room window. The trail that led from me to it was smooth and well-skied and glittering in the moonlight, and the fresh-blown powder snow made one long graceful sweep right up to that huge fourteen-by-fourteen-foot square of glass.

The house was lit like New Year's Eve.

He hadn't even bothered to draw the curtains. Why should he? After all, there was nothing higher up on Snowmass than the Austin Pierce house.

Except me.

I arched myself up and leaned around the side of the toboggan. It was quite a sight.

Now I knew why nobody had come looking for me.

Hank Wyland was obviously enjoying himself. He had a

drink in one hand and his police revolver in the other. Hank stood with his back to the big window, talking, smiling. I could see the top of Austin Pierce's bald head where he sat in one of the big leather chairs, just to the right of where Hank was standing.

The gun pointed at three people.

Al Coggin and Billy Medina, together at last, sat tense and white-faced on the big sofa. And Martha Ross stood behind them, pale as they were, wearing that same dark red hostess gown she'd worn Friday night, a million years ago.

I didn't know what Hank was saying, but it was easy to see from the look on their faces what the effect was.

They were getting ready to die.

I stared down at this pretty spectacle, at the five of them in that big expensive room, looking over the clean moonlit snow streaked with purple shadows.

I took a very deep breath then, and let it come out slow. Because all of a sudden I was very tired. Tired in a way that had only a little to do with what had happened to me on Snowmass this day, and how I'd worked my way down the mountain. I was morally tired. Tired of it all, of all the killing and conspiracies, the deceptions, the false faces. I was tired, bone-weary from being dragged against my will into this swamp of death and treachery, dragged on the kite strings of dreams dreamt by a long-gone seventeen-year-old kid named Joe Bird from Eagle Grove, Kansas.

I looked down across the ski slope at them, framed by the bright square of window, lit like actors on a stage, seen from far away, seen from the cheap seats.

I'd been in the cheap seats long enough.

I looked down at them and wanted nothing more than the end of it all. That was all the feeling left in me. There wasn't even anger anymore, at least not mainly, not the great hot rush of rage I had been feeling. It wasn't anger, or pain, not love or hate or courage. I simply wanted it all to stop, to stop then and for good.

I took another deep breath, not thinking it might be my last. Not thinking at all, maybe.

The resolution made itself, and from then on it was easy.

Here it comes, a little surprise package from Joe Bird to all you sons of bitches. I flexed my fucked-up right leg instinctively and with what might have been the last burst of real energy left in me I gave a good hard shove against the moonlit snowbank.

And between the slope of the trail and the momentum of my pushing, the old toboggan worked up quite a head of steam.

There was no dragging of legs now, no holding back.

Now I was moving fast, faster, making a grating noise, although nobody in the house seemed to hear me. My toboggan raced down the slope, and I shifted my weight to the left a little, aiming for the precise center of that window. The toboggan lurched a little, correcting its course. A collision course. Please, God, I thought, let's not spill, not here, not now.

We didn't spill.

The toboggan picked up more speed, and more on top of that, flying now, a bullet-shaped thing coming into its own, self-propelled now, big and fast and deadly.

Shaped like a bullet. That was my last thought as I lifted my head just enough to make sure we were on target, racing across the slope and up the small bank of windswept powder to the big plate-glass window.

The window got brighter and brighter and less and less real as it came racing at me. Then the sense of speed turned into a kind of weird slow motion, hypnotic, fascinating to the point where I nearly forgot to duck down behind the high metal prow of the toboggan for some small measure of safety.

But I did remember, finally, and crouched low as I could get myself as the big toboggan sailed gloriously up the snowbank and right through the window to the thunderous accompaniment of screaming and crashing glass and gunshots.

A bullet from Joe Bird, you bastards.

13

I was hearing voices again.

"He's dead."

It was Billy Medina's voice, dry and matter-of-fact even if it was lying.

I opened my eyes then, and realized Billy wasn't talking about me.

Hank Wyland lay on the shaggy white rug in front of the fire, his muscular neck twisted at a very peculiar angle. Hank was dead, and now I was twice a murderer. Hank would be leaving no more ski bums maimed and alone on Snowmass.

I had apparently rolled out of the toboggan when it landed. I was sprawled on the floor not far from Wyland, my broken left leg splayed out in its splint, the right leg twisted under me, my head against the side of the toboggan. I was too numb to hurt.

Both Al Coggin and Martha had acquired handguns. Billy was bending over what remained of Hank. Austin Pierce stood sputtering, trying against very uneven odds to regain some kind of control.

"I simply don't understand, who is this person . . . ?" Pierce was rambling, searching for the right tone. He never found it.

"You killed Blake." Martha said it simply, stating a fact. "He thought there was some kind of a plot. I told him it wasn't possible. Not from you. Not from my beloved Uncle Austin."

"Martha, honey . . . baby . . . you have to believe me . . ."

I could feel the panic rising in the man, and I won't try to kid you by pretending I didn't enjoy the spectacle. Even though I knew Pierce hadn't actually killed Blake Ross.

I looked at Pierce.

I've seen more than enough trapped animals. They all look the same. First they freeze. Then their eyes begin flicking about wildly, looking for ways out. Then they do something desperate. Pierce was in transition, from flicking to desperate. He looked at Martha with genuine wonderment, the kind of surprise that only the truly arrogant can know when their plans go wrong.

"Honey," he began, trying to control a voice that kept sliding away from him into panic, "Blake was right, I'd never in all my born days think of such a thing. Now, Martha, child, why don't you just give me that ugly thing?"

He began sidling closer to her. His right hand was out, reaching for the gun. His lips were forming words and rejecting them, moving silently as he groped for the magic phrase that would make her give him the gun.

She gave it to him.

The shots came fast and in precise order, three of them, at close range. Martha didn't move a muscle.

Austin Pierce fell screaming; then the screams turned to a gurgling. And then they stopped altogether.

Martha looked down at the gun in her hand with a kind of surprised distaste, as if it were a not very welcome present from a distant relative. Then she set it down on a table carefully and looked at Billy. "Joe Bird needs help, Captain."

By this time I was seeing things in a weird kind of slow motion. Martha walked toward me, knelt, and I felt more than saw her hand touching my forehead. My eyes closed then, and all I could feel was the warmth of the room and the cool touch of Martha's hand. There was no light and very little sound, and almost no feeling other than numbness and a vast echoing emptiness in my heart that felt like nothing and no one could ever fill it up again.

There is a place between waking and sleeping that sometimes seems more pleasant than either.

I don't know how long I was out, or if they'd given me anything for the pain, but at some point consciousness came drifting slowly, very slowly back at me. I wasn't sure I wanted it.

My eyes stayed mercifully shut. My mind stayed blank as I could make it.

I didn't want to think what demons might come riding

back on consciousness, didn't want to see what might or might not be left of me, didn't want to remember all the things I'd never forget.

Martha with that gun, for instance. The neck of Hank Wyland as he lay on the rug. Austin Pierce gurgling like an infant, sinking into death.

I was in a clean bed.

What I felt was flatness and cool. The flat under me and the cool around me. Flat on my back I lay, on cool sheets, pillow cool behind my head, hands folded across my chest outside the blanket, just waiting for the lily.

That isn't the way you sleep, Joe Bird. You sleep on your side, in your skin, not in some crazy nightshirt, not on your back, not with a pillow but with a lady. I was definitely not in my own bed. If I opened my eyes I might know where I was. I might establish a fact.

It was too much effort.

A sound, a click, a swishing-sliding noise. A door opening somewhere. And footsteps. A metallic sort of sound, the sound of something being set down. A tray, set on a table. A metallic clinking, a swoosh of fabric. Through resolutely closed eyelids I could feel the room get brighter. Someone had pulled back a curtain. A sudden warmth on my hands. A hand, a cool hand, but not so cool as Martha's hand, touched my forehead. We were getting quite a rash of forehead-touchers in Aspen these days. You never knew when they'd strike next. Practically an epidemic. Then the cool hand found its way to my wrist. Someone was taking liberties with my person. It tickled.

I smiled, hoping the hand and its owner would go away. For about a month.

"Well," said an unfamiliar but nevertheless female voice, "good morning, Mr. Bird."

The last person to call me Mr. Bird was a wanted criminal. I opened my eyes. A girl, starchy white uniform, a nurse, brown hair, pink-and-white face, a little plump but not bad, a good smile, glasses. Looked like she knew her job.

"Good morning."

She smiled some more and wheeled a mobile table to my bedside. There was a breakfast tray on it. Juice, coffee, eggs, sausage, cereal. I realized that starvation was imminent.

"You're looking better today."

"Thanks. What day is it?"

"Friday. You've been out for two days."

Two days. Not nearly long enough.

I sat up, and in sitting up noticed the huge cast on my left leg. At least I had a left leg. I wiggled and twitched a little, just to check out the systems. They were more or less in order. Then I looked at the nurse, who was watching me like an exhibit at the zoo. Well she might have.

"You're going to be fine."

"I'll take your word for it. Can I have visitors?"

"I think so. You have had, anyway. Rita Tyler's been here practically all the time. And Mrs. Ross. And the sheriff. And that boy who works for you."

"Rick?"

"That's him."

"How's Charlie?"

"The boy with the explosion burns? Much better. He's been asking for you, too."

So that much of my small world was still intact. I wondered about Gart, if he would still be lurking around somewhere waiting for a chance to pounce. I thought not.

"Tell me," I asked quietly, "how I really am."

I got a big serving of smile again. "You're a lot better than you have any right to be. The break's at least a clean break. It should set well. But there is some bad frostbite on the left foot. We're still worried about the big toe. It may come back. We're watching it very closely. If . . . well, that's for the doctor to say. And he'll be here later on this morning. But, basically, you're okay."

"Thanks."

I was better than okay.

I was alive. And measured by what had been flying at me these last days, that was so much better than okay, it amounted to a miracle.

I went through that breakfast like a ski through powder.

"What," I asked her, "is your name?"

"Marjorie."

"Marjorie, how about helping a helpless man and getting me another one of these?" I gestured at the empty tray.

"I think that can be arranged." She left to do it, and no

sooner had Marjorie departed than Sheriff Billy and Al Coggin came marching in, happy as hogs in new mud.

"He's up," said Billy, ever observant. He came over and shook my hand, very formal, and Al did the same. "Hail, the conquering hero," Billy went on. "You really saved our asses, Joe. Thanks."

"Wound up the whole case for us," Al chimed in.

"Yes, and I nearly wound it up for myself, too, looks like."

"You look fine, Joe." Al and Billy just stood there, grinning like fools.

"Funny, I don't feel fine. And what are you two grinning about?"

"Hell, Joe, we're just glad you're better. The doctor says you'll really be okay."

Outside, maybe, thank you very much, Billy. Inside, don't take any bets you can't afford to lose.

"Maybe," I said, trying to keep what little might be left of my cool, "you can tell me what, exactly, happened out there."

"You don't know?" Al started grinning all over again.

"I've been sleeping like a hop toad in winter for two days now. And I only knew my side of the thing anyhow, and not much of that."

"Well," said Billy, sitting in the room's only chair, thus establishing his preeminence over Al, "you came flying through that window like the angels of the Lord. Never did see a prettier sight."

"Thanks, Billy. I think you're pretty, too."

"You probably want to know why he had a gun on us." Al broke into Billy's narrative. As usual. Assassins may come and toes may go, but Medina and Coggin will quarrel on forever.

"Well, your girl called us, Rita, you know."

I knew.

"She said about Hank Wyland's phone call, and how you were going up the mountain, and all, and so we went right out there, naturally, and then—"

"We thought to check at the Pierce place, just in case you'd all gotten back down the hill already, and—"

"Him"—Billy gestured at Al, whom he had never been

known to call by name—"and me knocked at the door, and there they all were."

"Mrs. Ross, big as life and not hurt at all, and—"

"Wyland and Pierce, none of 'em claiming to know anything about any phone call to you, Joe."

"So they kept you there by force?"

"No, they offered us drinks, and we had one."

"Where did the gun come from?"

"Well, you see, Rita called again. Very worried. Suggested we get up a night search—"

"And we were going to do that, Joe—"

"That was when Wyland got aggressive."

"Began saying you were in on the plot somehow."

"Mrs. Ross wasn't having any of that."

"Wyland got madder and madder."

"Pretty soon he was holding his gun on us."

"What," I asked, "do you think he intended to do with it? Kill you all?"

"I guess we may never know that."

"It was right about then you came through the window."

"Neither of them admitted anything?"

"I'd say," said Billy, "that pulling that gun was an admission."

"And Pierce? How do you fit him into it?"

"Why, he had to be the ringleader. The brains. The financing. It's doubtful that he did any of the dirty work himself, though."

His work was dirty enough for me, and for Blake, and Martha.

"I take it," I asked, "that no one will be preferring charges against Mrs. Ross."

"Self-defense, pure and simple."

I guess it was, at that.

We chatted on for a few minutes more, Al and Billy told me the inquest was pending my testimony, that it could all be done right here in the hospital room because it looked like I'd be there for a couple of weeks at the least, what with the break and the frostbite and a couple of other things.

Then they left, at almost the exact time Nurse Marjorie appeared with my second breakfast. I wolfed it down, too. I'd earned it.

Martha, I'd learned from Billy, was still in town.

She'd blacked out right after shooting Pierce. When she came out of it, Martha couldn't face the thought of another night in Pierce's house. She was in town, at the Aspen Inn. They didn't know anything of her plans.

I figured I'd find out soon enough.

They'd never found the body in the Colorado River. Gart had vanished altogether. I still didn't know how O'Leary died, or what, precisely, he'd been so fatally right about.

I wasn't sure I wanted to know the answer to that one. Even thinking about it had a way of bringing me trouble. Then I heard her voice.

"Hi."

The room got warmer then, but not from the rising sun. I looked up. Rita stood in the doorway, the long gold hair glowing, a smile trembling on her lips. She walked across the little hospital room, fast, and bent to kiss me. And got egg on her sweater.

"You've got egg on your sweater." Joe Bird, ever smooth, brimming with romantic speeches.

"You've got rocks in your head." She kissed me again. It was a feeling you could get used to. Any number of times.

"I know. You told me not to go."

"I told you something else, too." She sat next to the bed and held my hand. My depraved mind instantly began figuring out *Popular Mechanics* techniques for having sex in a cast. I was feeling better, after all.

"I remember." I remembered very well. And I wasn't brave enough to face what she'd said, not just then, not in that room, trapped in that hunk of plaster, surrounded on all sides by bad memories and unanswered questions. Rita must have sensed this: anyway, she didn't press the issue.

We talked casually after that, talked about Charlie, who was making an unexpectedly good recovery. The doctor said they'd be able to give him walking therapy in a few days, that he'd be out of the hospital altogether in maybe a couple of more weeks if everything kept on going well. I might be out in two weeks too, with luck.

There was a knock on the door.

"Come in."

"The refreshment committee," said Rick, grinning from ear

to ear, "has arrived." He was carrying a huge paper bag that proved to contain French bread and three cheeses and two bottles of red wine plus wineglasses from Joe's Place and a red-checkered napkin. It was a little soon after my two breakfasts, but I joined them in a glass of wine anyway.

Rick told me about Joe's Place. It seemed a thousand miles away and years ago in time. They were doing fine. I expected that. Finally they both left, taking the remains of the picnic on to Charlie, promising to come back later in the day, in relays. Rita kissed me as she left, squeezed my hand. *Rita loved me.* That changed all the rules, whatever the old rules had been. I tried to remember them, and couldn't.

I finished the wine and stretched as much as I could with the cast, and all of a sudden felt sleepy. I closed my eyes, just for a minute.

When I woke up, twilight had taken me by surprise. I looked at my watch: the nap had lasted five hours.

Captain Richards knocked on my door and walked right in. He came up to the bed, shook my hand, and smiled. Not very convincingly. "I . . . we . . . owe you a mighty big apology, Joe."

I was beyond grinding axes. "Forget it. Nobody owes anybody in this game, Captain. Nobody knew the rules, nobody had a scorecard."

"They damn near killed you. That's what I meant."

"I noticed."

"I trusted Wyland. I would have trusted him with the wife, the kids, anything."

"Anyone would. It wasn't your fault."

Richards sighed, a good man with a bagful of trouble. When he spoke again, it was almost as though I wasn't there, as though he were trying, and not for the first time, to talk himself into something.

"You know," he began, softly, "when they killed Jack Kennedy, and all those conspiracy theories came popping up like mushrooms after rain, I kind of laughed at them—crackpots, I thought, maybe because we see so many crazies in our work. I mean look at Lassiter; innocent, but nutty in his own way. But if this is what it smells like, if someone went to all the trouble of planting Hank Wyland with us . . ." His voice trailed off.

"Maybe Hank wasn't a plant. People can change. People can get a little drunk with power, maybe, they can get to a point where the law moves too slowly, to where they want to speed it up a little."

"This isn't a good man being overzealous, Joe. Four people are dead."

"Maybe five."

I told him what little I knew about Robert O'Leary. He listened in silence.

"God. And nobody else knows?"

"Nobody connected with the law, Captain. Things were moving pretty fast there for a while, and I was respecting the lady's wishes: she's been through enough, wouldn't you say?"

"I'll see what I can do." Defeat crept into his voice as he said it. "It's too neat, Joe, too resolved. We can't ask Pierce, or Wyland either."

"Or O'Leary."

"The trouble is, with both of them dead, it's unprovable. There's no confession. We may never know more than we do right now."

"Which is to say not very much?"

"Which is to say zero. We know who, but we don't know beans about why."

"How about Gart?"

"Disappeared. Could be anywhere by now. I'm not betting we'll find him."

"Then there's no trial, no testimony."

"People are moving right now, Joe, and it makes me madder than a sidewinder on hot tar to think about it, to cover up the whole mess, play it like it never happened."

"Welcome to Skigate. You mean, they'll let a guy like Blake Ross get murdered and just sweep the whole thing under the rug?"

"It may be allowed to die a slow death, and there isn't really one goddamn thing we can do about it. What could we prove?"

"Ross died of a broken heart? Who's going to buy that one?"

"Austin Pierce had a lot of powerful friends, Joe."

"Some more alive than others. It was a pretty risky business, being a friend of Austin Pierce."

I looked out the window. The blue afternoon sky was racing itself through the spectrum on its way to purple.

"I'm only mentioning it, Joe, because I know you care."

"I care. I guess."

I cared more than anyone was ever likely to find out. And being helpless to do anything about the whole mess made me care still more.

"If I can think of anything to do, I'll do it."

"I'm sure of that."

"Meanwhile, take care of yourself."

"Can't do a whole lot else, can I? Thanks for coming by."

He was a good man, an honest one. He meant well. And I hated him for not having all the answers, for not trying harder, for not doing the impossible.

"So long, Joe."

"So long."

Now I'd had every visitor but the one I wanted most, and feared the most. I lay in bed seething with the restlessness of an active man trapped in stillness and seething with other, more complicated feelings too. In one way or another, I'd spent most of my life waiting for Martha. A few hours more shouldn't have mattered. They did.

Her knock when it came was like many things about Martha: quiet and decisive.

"Joe?"

It was a good question. I'd been wondering who I was too, and who I was turning into—who or what.

"You *are* better. I'm so glad. You had us worried."

She still said "us." Blake was that much a part of her. Martha walked into my room, pale and quiet in the darkening light. I sat up, smiled. It was just like old times. Just like the old times that never were, that would never be again, even in dreaming. I would have dreams, maybe, but not that particular dream. I'd lost that dream somewhere in the cold night on Snowmass Mountain.

"Hi," I said, ever profound. "You didn't wake me, Martha. Seems I've been asleep for two days steady. How are you?"

She came to my bedside and sat down, and took my hand. Her hand was cool. "Shaky. I guess we both have reason to be shaky, Joe. It's like a very bad nightmare."

"Nightmares have an advantage: you wake up."

"Yes." Her voice wandered off, then came back. "I've lived a thousand years this week."

"It's over."

"I keep telling myself that. It doesn't seem to make a whole lot of difference, Joe."

"You may be still in shock. Have you seen a doctor?"

"That night. The night you came through the window. He gave me tranquilizers."

Maybe it was a pill that gave her voice that strange, slightly unfocused quality. Or maybe it was fear, or simple fatigue.

"Would you like a glass of wine?"

"Sure. I mean, I don't usually take wine, but, yes. Sure."

I poured us each half a glass of Stag's Leap Cabernet. When Rick raids the wine cellar, he raids good.

I raised my glass. "To . . . the future."

"Yes," she said, a little spark coming back into that faraway voice. "That's a good thought. The future."

Our glasses made a lonely little clink, a small brave noise, but not enough to drive away the wolves that were circling the campfire.

"What will you do?"

"It's unlike me, Joe, but I almost haven't been able to think about that." She sipped the wine. "I still see him. I still hear the gun. See the blood."

"You mean Pierce."

"He would have killed us also."

"Probably. Or his sidekick. He liked to leave the dirty work to Wyland."

"The police have been very kind."

I tasted my wine and looked at her over the top of the glass. And I thought how easy it was to be kind to Martha.

"They know what you've been through."

"That was the unreal part, when it finally dawned on me that Uncle Austin was behind it all. I've known him all my life, Joe. He was like one of the family. When he came at me, and I knew I'd have to shoot, it was like it wasn't me at all pulling the trigger."

"You did it very well."

"He might have been a mad dog."

"Something like that."

"But tell me about you, Joe. The leg. What does your doctor say? You looked pretty bad when you came through that window."

"The doctor says I'll be fine. At the very worst, I might lose a toe, but that's unlikely. It's you I'm worried about."

"That is sweet of you, Joe Bird. But you always were sweet to me, weren't you? There is a lot to be done. Naturally, life doesn't just stop."

"Life," I said, quoting Rita in quite another context, "goes on."

"Yes. I have no home now, not really. Not Eagle Grove. I could stay in Philadelphia, or even Washington. But I'm just not sure. Someone hinted—mind you, just hinted—at the funeral, that I might take over his seat in the Senate, you know, an interim appointment, then run for the vacancy next term. But I rather think not. I am more of a behind-the-scenes person. They mean well, but it seems I can be more useful in other ways."

"You have always done a lot for other people."

"I try. You see, Joe, I don't intend to let Blake's ideals die with him. The things he stood for, well, they will still need someone to stand up for them."

Her voice was stronger now, feeding on the force of her belief in what Blake stood for. A new look came into Martha's eye, a hint of fire. It was easy to imagine her leading regiments of horsemen to the coronation of the Dauphin at Rheims, following the Voices only she could hear.

"I understand."

"It's hard, Joe. For one thing, there's all that money. Daddy's money and Blake's. He was very rich."

"I didn't know that."

"What I'm most interested in is some kind of library, a living memorial. And of course scholarships. Maybe a chair in political science somewhere. . . ."

There might have been a smoother way to ask the question I had to ask at that moment. If there was, I didn't know about it. So I just marched right on in, barefoot through the jungle. "Martha, can I ask you a question?"

"Why, sure."

"What did you do with the gun?"

There was a pause, then a quiet sound as she set her wineglass down on my bedside table.

Martha's clear gray eyes were on mine. She didn't react with her face, or give any other indication that she'd heard me. Then slowly her eyes darkened, as though a cloud were passing over the sun. The pause seemed to last for a very long time.

Finally she spoke. The words came out gently, measured, as if in a dream. "The year we were married, Blake Ross and I, a young man came to call on Blake. A tall, sad, awkward young man. I gave them tea, then left them alone together. Later, oh, perhaps two hours later, I ran into the young man as he was leaving. You would have had to be there, Joe, to see the change in him. Total. He was quite a different person. He even walked differently, proudly. It was as if the whole direction of his life had changed, and for the better. In that short time. Later, and I won't go into the details, I found out that his life had changed. You see, that young man had a dream. And he'd just about given up on it. Blake gave him new faith in his dream, in himself. People were always bringing Blake Ross their dreams. He had that power. He could take someone's tired old wreck of a dream and patch it all up and put it into focus and send it off into the world to grow and flourish. Blake Ross had magic, Joe. He could change things, and people too." She smiled, remembering.

"Was that a reason to kill him?"

Martha looked across the bed at me. A kind of gentle astonishment floated across her face, incredulity that I could be so dense as to fail to understand her.

"It was," she said softly, affectionately, "the only way to save him."

"Save him?"

Martha was right to be astonished. I am dense.

"You don't understand. I was twenty-one when I met Blake. You should have seen him then, Joe. You should have heard him. The ideals he had. The dreams. He was magical, Joe. It was a special grace, an almost mystical power in him. I wasn't the only one who felt that, although maybe I felt it more strongly, more surely than most. You met him. There was still some of it left. Enough to keep up the facade."

"Then it was a facade?"

"It had turned into one, into the shell of what he had been, of what he could have become. There was a time when he could have gone anywhere, Joe, and done anything. And I shared that dream. He asked me to share it."

The dream. The sacred trust. More sacred even than life.

"So you married the dream?"

"I married the dream!" She said it triumphantly. "And saw it rot from inside. I saw Blake Ross fall in love with his own image, court power, get power as easily as he got women—oh, yes, and there were women, plenty of them, not that they meant anything to him, or to me either. They got to be just another one of his many perks, like the limousines and the press coverage. Rome wasn't destroyed in a day, Joe, nor was Blake Ross. It took years, and I watched it all from a ringside seat. Horrible. Watching someone you love slowly deteriorate."

She stood up then, and walked to the window. It was dark outside. Martha paused at the window, then turned and came back to my bedside and picked up her glass. She took a very small sip of wine, and continued. The fire had gone out of her voice now. It was soft, almost a whisper.

"At first, everything went well for us. You have to believe that."

I believed.

"We worked together. Oh, how we worked. And everything seemed to fall into place."

"It looked that way."

"Then, slowly, bit by bit, I began to understand exactly why certain things worked so well. The compromises. The selling out. The corruption."

"You mean he was crooked?"

"Not in the way the world thinks of crooked. Not in obvious black and white. No. He was honest, in terms of the law. It was his dream that he cheated on, Joe. It was all festering inside. Invisibly."

"Except to you."

"Except to me. Invisible and growing, just like cancer. But it wouldn't have stayed invisible much longer. Also like cancer. Power came so easily to him, Joe, that it was just natural he'd want more. Power is addictive. Well, there is nothing wrong with power if it's used to good ends. But

Blake got so that all he wanted was the power itself, the ability to manipulate people, to make things happen, to pull the strings. And at the end it was the very act of pulling those strings that fascinated him, not the results. He got so the lies would flow out of that beautiful mouth with the same sweet sincerity as truths or words of love, or . . ."

"That bad?"

"It was worse than you dream. I remember him laughing—laughing—at people who came to him because they believed, believed in Blake Ross the way I once did, the way that sad young man did. That was the worst. The mockery. And that, in the end, was what made me decide."

"But you weren't involved with Pierce, or that crew?"

She laughed then, a lilting, small girl's laugh. "The makers of martyrs? To think they would have done it for me. Irony is always waiting in the wings, isn't it?"

I couldn't argue that point.

"Who," I asked, "was O'Leary?"

If Martha noticed the past tense, she didn't show it. A lot of things were past tense for Martha now, and always would be.

"A nice young man who was completely taken in by Senator Blake Ross. A nice young man who had this crazy theory that some far-right Texans were actually getting up a conspiracy to kill my husband. It is," she said with a small frown, "the final irony that Austin Pierce wanted to kill Blake Ross the crusader, the dreamer of dreams. Blake had even taken them in. His act was that good. They were conspiring to kill a man who had been dead for years."

I noticed that my wineglass was empty, and refilled it. Martha had hardly touched hers.

"You always were a crack shot."

We might have been chatting about absent friends. It's hard to know what tone of voice works best when you're trying to get a girl you've dreamed of all your life to confess to murder. It was not a field in which I'd had lots of experience. There we were, me in the bed, Martha in her chair again, the both of us killers, both of our heads filled with questions that might be very much better unasked, questions that were going to get asked anyway.

I felt just about the way I'd felt in the ski-patrol toboggan rushing across the trail at Pierce's window: reckless now, beyond caring, somewhere between life and death, operating on raw nerve and gut instinct, beyond hope or logic or even fear.

Small lightning flashes of logic glittered across my brain at irregular intervals, charming little thoughts like: *maybe she'll kill me now, too, add another notch to her halo.* These thoughts came and went, and I didn't pay much attention to them. There didn't seem to be a great deal of point to it.

"Pierce," I suggested, "did your job for you, in any event."

"I don't think I get your meaning, Joe."

"Already they're beginning to hush the whole thing up. I'm sure you put the rifle where it won't be found."

"I think so."

"It was a rifle?"

"A Winchester model seventy. Thirty-oh-six." She stood up again. My eyes followed her to the window, and back to my bedside. She stood close to the bed now, a slender dark shape, backlit by the one lamp on the table by the window. She touched my cheek with her small cool hand. "I may sound crazy, Joe. I may be crazy. But I know what I did and why I did it, and I'm not afraid to answer for it. Naturally, it'll be a mess. Thank God we don't have any kids."

The "we" again. He was still alive for her, would always be more alive than anyone who merely walked on the earth and breathed its air.

"When we were seventeen, I was in love with you."

She didn't seem to hear me. "I don't know the penalities in this state."

"I remember a night, your daddy was having a party. There were lilacs."

"I probably won't even be able to plead madness."

"I'd never known anyone like you."

"In a way, I guess I am mad."

"It was years before I stopped dreaming about you."

"Joe, I am sorry. I haven't been listening."

"It wasn't important."

Her hand was still on my cheek. She had forgotten that, too. I reached up and covered it with my big, rough, half-bandaged hand.

"What were you saying, Joe?"

"Good-bye."

"Good-bye? Just like that?"

"I hope you'll be happy."

"Joe, that's just cruel. You never were one to play games. Don't start now."

Wrong, Martha. It was all a game. A charade, to be exact.

It was totally dark outside now. I still held her hand. There was no way to tell her exactly what I felt, because I didn't know myself. When the words did come, they were inadequate, like most words.

"Look," I said, slowly, as if translating from a foreign language, "I've killed two men this week. You've done the same. Does that put me in a position to judge you, or anyone, ever?"

"Am I hearing right?"

Her hand jerked convulsively under mine, then lay still. It was like a small animal, dying.

"The killers of Blake Ross are dead, Martha."

"Are you serious?"

"Serious as I'll ever be, God help me."

"But the trial . . ."

"What trial? There isn't going to be a trial. You can't try dead men."

"Joe. What'll I do?"

"You'll walk out of this room and get yourself back to the inn and pack. Tomorrow morning you'll be on the first plane out of here. And you'll go home, wherever home is going to be. And take your dream with you, yours and his. Maybe it's a good dream, Martha. I'm not qualified to tell."

"I hope it is. I hope it was worth it." Her hand moved out from under mine. I made no attempt to keep it. Martha bent down then, and kissed me on the cheek. It was a dry little kiss, a butterfly passing too close.

"Good-bye, Joe. I hope you're doing the right thing."

So did I.

"Shall I tell you my secret? There is no right thing, Martha. Not in this situation. My guess is, you'll do a lot more right things in your life than Joe Bird ever dreamed of. I've never been very big on dreams, you know. The best ones I ever had were small-town dreams. But you always wanted to change the world."

"I guess I did."

She turned away from me then, and walked to the window. But there was nothing to see from my window but darkness.

"Good-bye, Joe. Thank you."

"Good luck."

She walked out of my life silently, with that graceful dark head held high, slipped through the door and closed it after her without a sound, then vanished into the mountain darkness like the ghost of a half-remembered dream.

14

The snows came early this fall.

I missed the broadcast of the ground-breaking ceremonies for the Blake Ross Memorial Library at Princeton because something much more important happened that day.

The chair lift opened on Ajax Mountain.

Rita couldn't be with me, being nearly eight months pregnant with what we assume—from the way he kicks—will be Joe Junior. She's too busy these days anyway, fixing up the nursery in our new house on the ridge behind town.

Charlie has my old brass bed now. Charlie's the manager of Joe's Place, and doing damn well at it. The fact that half of his right foot is missing in no way interferes with Charlie's walking, or skiing, or the occupancy rate of my former bed, which, rumor has it, is booked to capacity. Charlie's all right. The only problem is, we can't ski together much, because when he isn't minding the store, I am.

The chair lift creaked and grumbled a little as it swept me up the mountain. The sky over Aspen was a happy mixture of blue and white, all changes and wind sounds and scudding clouds. The chair rose through the stands of pencil-thin aspen trees and on up through the giant spruce and over the great white bowls and meadows ripe with a fresh crop of powder snow. Soon I was on top of it all, on top of the world.

I skimmed off the lift a little gingerly. It was more of an event than just the first skiing day of the new winter.

It was my first day on skis since the incident on Snowmass last year. And however hard I tried to forget, however much Rita tried to make me forget, to give me other, better things to remember, the horror of that one mad week was part of me as much as the kid inside Rita was part of me, and like the kid, squirming, eager to get out.

There was no way of telling how much my mashed left leg would affect my skiing.

I stood there on top of Ajax looking down at the valley. The mountain's broad shoulders hide the town itself from where I stood, but I could see across the valley to the far ridge, and catch the dappled sunlight playing hide and seek with clouds, glinting merrily off the windows of my new house, then touching it with shadow. The doctor is on record as saying my left leg is as good as it ever was.

His optimism is touching.

But I feel good. I've been doing ski exercises ever since the cast came off, and on our honeymoon in Hawaii Rita and I did some surfing. Tricky but fun.

I stood on the side of the trail in the uncluttered air of Aspen and faked indecision about which trail I'd take. There really was no question: it'd be Gentleman's Ridge all the way. There was a certain pleasure just standing there in the glittering sunlight, anticipating the run.

I stood with all God's blue Rockies at my back and fingered the rip in my lucky red parka, neatly mended by Rita, torn while crashing Hank Wyland's little party at the Pierce house last season.

Last season. The time may come when I'll forget it. Don't hold your breath.

Maybe I stood there for five minutes, maybe less. It was long enough. Then I pushed off, skating a little at the start of it, out of sheer bravado, not knowing if the legs could still take it.

They took it and ran.

And it felt like it always feels, maybe better, for wanting it so much, the rush of it, the hiss of steel on snow, the lifting, soaring, gliding down this great permanent dream of a mountain, all unleashed and free and flying, flying.

I'll never learn.